EARTH SHIP PROTECTRESS

ALSO BY JOHN RICKS

Freddy Anderson's Home: Book 1 in the Freddy Anderson Chronicles (second edition)

Sword and Sorcery: Short Stories, Book 1

EARTH SHIP PROTECTRESS

BOOK TWO IN THE
Freddy Anderson Chronicles

BY

John RICKS

FREDDY ANDERSON CHRONICLES
EARTH SHIP PROTECTRESS

iUniverse books may be ordered through booksellers or by contacting:

iUniverse
1663 Liberty Drive
Bloomington, IN 47403
www.iuniverse.com
1-800-Authors (1-800-288-4677)

Because of the dynamic nature of the Internet, any web addresses or links contained in
this book may have changed since publication and may no longer be valid. The views
expressed in this work are solely those of the author and do not necessarily reflect the
views of the publisher, and the publisher hereby disclaims any responsibility for them.

Any people depicted in stock imagery provided by Thinkstock are models,
and such images are being used for illustrative purposes only.
Certain stock imagery © Thinkstock.

ISBN: 978-1-4917-7985-9 (sc)
ISBN: 978-1-4917-7986-6 (e)

Library of Congress Control Number: 2015917717

Print information available on the last page.

iUniverse rev. date: 02/09/2016

To children everywhere. May you be
the heroes you were born to be.

INTRODUCTION

✦ ✦ ✦

The aliens continue to search Freddy's mind to find out how he destroyed their greatest ship. The world finds out about the Earth-destroying disaster that is about to happen and panics, and Freddy finds out that the disaster was not what he thought; it's worse. Freddy starts the world on a course that will either spiral out of control or rescue the human race from itself. Will Freddy succeed? Time will tell. If he doesn't, life as you know it will never be the same.

P R O L O G U E

✦ ✦ ✦

I can't say I awoke. It was more like I was allowed to think. I was again immersed in thick, clear liquid, and green translucent tentacles held my body in the center of a tank. My energy was still drained, but something was different. I could feel emotions again—just a little, but they were there—and they were alien.

I remember many things that I did not know before. It was as if someone was feeding me information about this race of beings—how great they were, how impossible it would be to fight against them, and how much it would benefit my people if we surrendered to them and became their allies.

Then it hit me—their minds leak! I saw what being their "allies" would mean. Allies? "Slaves" was more like it! They wanted us for our technology and then as frontline fodder for some of their wars. Now that I was aware, I could hear voices and see the Green.

✦

Green said in a booming voice, "Something is different."
Gray asked, "What?"

Everything went black, but the voices and emotions continued.

Green answered, "Master, sire. He is aware."

I sensed Gray stumble back a step; all four of his weapons were quickly pulled and pointed at the tank and my head, and his eyes went so wide I thought they would pop out. Gray turned to his men. "If the creature becomes fully aware, kill it!"

Blue calmly asked, "Can he use his powers?"

The Green answered, "No, sire."

"Then there is nothing to worry about. Gray, cancel that order! Green, start the process."

Gray answered, "As you wish, sire." He turned to someone and said, "Stand down on that last."

Green said, "Yes, sire. By the way, how did your meeting with the Whites go?"

"I told the Whites what I wanted them to know. They are sending that information back to their respective media counterparts on their planets. Please start."

✦ ✦ ✦

CANNIBALS

What a time I've had. My home is finally built; it's wonderful and works great. My home. My canyon. It's a good feeling to have that part of the work completed. Mom and Dad always wanted a Victorian home. Tears come to my eyes, so I stop thinking about how much I miss them. Everything I'd planned is going great so far. The computer system is working better than expected, and so are the defenses. I did not start out wanting defenses, but the nasty old army guys forced me to rethink that issue. It was the army that made me see the need for my babysitters. I have babysitters. What a mess! Instead of being by myself, I've a dozen women guarding me night and day. Good thing too, as I'm at war with the media. That worries me the most. There is a brighter side. I have my first girlfriend. Becky is the most beautiful girl in the world. I really need to find the time to see her more often. She was somewhat upset with my not contacting her.

SEAL team leader Lieutenant Susan is the one in charge of my safety now. Smart woman. Maybe a little too smart for me. She believes she played me like a fish on an unbreakable line. I'm a super genius, but my talent is geared toward inventing, not handling people. I'm rather ignorant in that area. Susan is a genius in handling people and knows exactly how to control me. In addition, most of the time I don't even know she's doing it! I'm having a lot of fun playing with her.

Another one of the SEAL team members is Katie. She's telepathic like me. Susan uses her to check on me when I'm working. She's a great person.

Now that the press conferences are over, I need to get back to work. Keeping my mind clear is going to be hard, but I need to keep it clear because I don't have time to waste—not if I'm going to save the world from destruction.

"Stop!"

Not everything went black. The room was sharp in my mind, and so were the occupants. The Green, Gray, and Blue were close by. There were three other Greens monitoring equipment. There were also seventeen other Grays and eight Purples. They must consider me dangerous, or they're protecting Gray from Blue. Blue is acting aloof, but he is worried.

✦

Blue said, "There it is again. Something is threatening his world! Probe hard each time this comes up. We need to know."

"Yes, sire. He is fighting again."

"Don't fight him. Feed him information."

"Yes, sire."

✦

I went to my workshop to concentrate and start the next phase of my plan. Three days later, I came out. I was hungry, and the computer tactfully informed me that the lieutenant was getting very insistent that I come out for something to eat. When I exited the shop, the lieutenant came outside with half the crew.

"Anything wrong, Lieutenant?"

"No, Freddy. I just don't like your being gone that long without seeing you or hearing from you."

"Now, Lieutenant, Katie has been checking on me regularly, and I'm sure she told you I was doing fine. Her mental touch is getting stronger, now that she's using it more."

"Don't try to change the subject on me, young man. You get into that house, take a bath for goodness' sake, and come down for dinner. You're going to go to bed right after that. You look like you're about to drop."

"Yes, ma'am. It's because of that issue I mentioned. I'm rearranging my priorities in building right now. It's a lot of work, but I'm on my way. Anything happen while I was working?"

She pointed me toward the house and started walking that way with me. "More supplies came in."

"Already?"

"Yes. And your replacement generators are in. I took the liberty of having them flown here." I looked around, saw where they were, and started toward them. She put her hands on my shoulders and pointed me back toward the house. "You can play with them tomorrow. Tonight, you're doing exactly as I say."

"Thank you for bringing in the supplies, Susan."

"You're welcome. Mr. Zimmer called and said that the people you're prosecuting went to court and pleaded guilty to all charges. It's all over the news. They're going to have the sentencing tomorrow morning."

"That was fast."

"Mr. Zimmer said they want to talk but want this out of

the way first. He also said that the government has shut down twenty-three newspapers and magazines and one television station. They've pressed charges against over eighty others and expect to close down a few major companies soon."

"I thought that you could not revoke an advertising license. How are they shutting them down? Isn't that causing a big freedom-of-the-press issue?"

"Many of their licenses have come due or were coming due. The government is simply refusing to renew until all charges are over with. They've arrested hundreds of people because of your investigations. Mr. Zimmer took out advertisements on each major channel to detail what the media had done and how badly they had led the public to believe things that simply weren't true. He also leaked to each newspaper about the other, and they sensationalized it so much that everyone is in an uproar over the whole thing. Even the media is upset with the media. Several cities have had demonstrations against the self-proclaimed 'news professionals,' and a few people have been hurt. There's talk in Washington about making laws that will crack down on them and force them to be scrupulously honest. They won't take away their first-amendment right of free speech, as this great country is founded on that, but they will make it very painful to knowingly print lies, half-truths, and misleading information that will harm others. With a good lie detector in place, the government will know when it's malicious. Companies could end up completely out of business if they don't comply."

"Lieutenant, let's be realistic. The government has tried this many times before and failed. No law has been passed yet, and talk, especially in Washington, is real cheap. The media is probably sucking up all of this and selling more papers than ever. People watch television more than ever, and the riots are just something else to report. The fact that they would report on each other just shows their cannibalistic tendencies, and the 'hundreds of arrests' have not been prosecuted yet. We're doing them a favor, and that's not what I wanted. We need to cost them money because that's the only thing they understand."

"That's the best part. The estimated number of subscriptions either canceled or not renewed is in the tens of millions. The television ratings for the news have dropped way down, and they've lost most of their sponsors. No one is watching the news except for a few shows that have a reputation for reporting the truth. You're costing them big bucks. An independent group funded by the government has been installed to rate the accuracy of each news group, based on fairness, honesty, and completely unbiased stories. The surprise and hatred that erupted after their first report, which showed less than 50 percent accuracy in their stories and even less fairness across the board, is what caused the riots. People are totally disgusted, and they've stopped watching."

"We'll see what happens. I can hope for the best, but I'm not expecting much."

I took my shower, and it felt great. I had no idea how bad I'd smelled until I picked up my clothes to put them down the laundry chute. I washed my hands after touching my dirty clothes. Dinner was great, and I would have stuffed myself, but Colleen made me "slow down and chew." After dinner, I took the time to write a letter to Becky. I missed her, and I wanted to know all about what she was doing. I fell asleep at my desk in my room. Katie did a mental check on me and came up to put me in bed and tuck me in.

✦

"This is confusing."

Things started to go black but did not completely get there.

Both Green and Gray said, "Sire?"

"Why would the media be inaccurate? Our Whites report to an exactness that is nearly unbelievable."

Green said, "Our Whites are fanatics about accuracy. If they find one of their own reporting something inaccurately, they are stoned to death. American species of Whites— or media, as they call them—have legal protection at the highest level that allows them to lie. They are paid on what they report. If they do not have a story, then they get no money and cannot eat. Therefore, they also have incentive to lie. The good reporters, the vast majority, do not have to worry, as they work hard and can find stories, but it seems that the few bad reporters make up stories, tell pointless stories worded to make them look like real news, or report in such a way as to draw emotions from others, which sometimes ruins the lives of the ones they report on. It is called entertainment. I have had several in my tanks that literally hate the Whites, yet they would use them for their own ends if needed. Because of these few, the many Whites are distrusted."

"You say this is only in one group? And how do they tell entertainment from real news?"

"Yes, sire. As far as we know at this time, it is only one group. They cannot tell which is real."

"Sad, that is."

Gray said, "Something for the Yellows to straighten out if we retain this species as allies."

Blue telepathically whispered, "*Or the Blacks.*"

Fear instantly struck the other two, and Green stammered, "Perhaps—perhaps I need to con ... continue."

CHAPTER 2

FAITH

"Freddy. *Freddy!*"

"Yes?"

"Shop wants a word with you."

"Patch her through."

"Good morning, Freddy. I was watching the completion of the hull and determined that the work should stop what my sensors determined is a mistake."

"What mistake?"

"I believe you wanted to install an engine into this machine. Is that correct?"

"Yes, of course."

"There is no place to put it."

I was still in bed, covered up nice and warm, but I quickly sat up and threw the covers off. "Whoops! I'll be there as soon as I can."

"After breakfast. You don't want the lieutenant mad at you again, do you?"

"Good idea. Thanks."

"You're welcome, Freddy."

It was after seven when I made it downstairs. As I walked into the kitchen, Colleen, covered in flour, had just set my breakfast down on the table—pancakes with blueberries and bacon chips, good and hot. Yum! More bacon was sizzling on the stove top, and something that smelled very good was in the oven. Colleen's having breakfast ready for me made me think Katie was using her telepathic ability a little more than I expected, but it wasn't causing me any problems, so I let it go.

"Good morning, Colleen."

"Good morning, Freddy. Have a nice sleep?"

"Yes, I did. You know, I really don't mean to work for so long without talking to anyone. I'm sorry."

"Cheer up. That's the nature of the beast, Freddy. For every action, there is a reaction. For every gift, there is a price to pay. For everything that happens, there is a repercussion. You're gifted, and so you pay for it with being drifty." She laughed and tousled my long hair.

"Katie is gifted, and she pays for it by being able to hear what she doesn't want to hear."

"You eat, and then you have to use the restroom at some point."

"So what you're telling me is that for anything you do, there is something that happens because of it. My professors called it cause and effect."

"Not all things are bad, Freddy. You bake a cake; someone gets to eat it. You fall in love with someone, and someone may fall in love with you. Some reactions are good. We just need to sit back and ask ourselves, 'If I do this or that, what will the reaction be? Will it be worth it? Will it be good not only in the short term but also in the long term?' For most of us, it makes very little difference what we do, as it affects very little. You, on the other hand, have the ability to affect everyone on this planet. When I was very young, my father sat me down and told me this. He said he was one of the lucky ones—what he did made little difference."

"I disagree. He had you, and you're making a lot of difference to me."

"That's sweet, Freddy, but he was saying that he felt sorry for the ones who are destined to change the world. They take a lot of people with them, and the souls of many rest upon their shoulders. Everything they do affects everyone else, and they will be held responsible in the eyes of God. Do you believe in God, Freddy?"

I looked at her with tears starting to develop in my eyes. Fear of God and the possible reactions if you don't do as told would cause anyone to be afraid. "If you could read minds and receive as strongly as I can, you would have no choice. It takes no faith when you know he's there."

She looked startled and leaned in closer. "Freddy, have you ever talked to God?"

I looked at her and said nothing, but she could see the worry in my face. "Colleen, if you knew there was a God, and you knew that he wanted you to do something—say, like making space travel possible—what would happen if you refused?"

"I would not refuse anything that God wanted me to do, Freddy. But if I did, I would expect God to take vengeance on me and mine. God loves us very much, but he does get angry when we don't obey him."

"I don't think he gets mad very much, but he …" I stopped to think how I could say this without sounding like I was crazy. "I mean, conversationally speaking, yes, he does love us … very, very much. I'd also say he laughs a lot at the predicaments we get ourselves into." I looked up at the ceiling with a disapproving look and said, "I'll bet he likes to watch us fall in love and rolls all over heaven with laughter when we get kissed unexpectedly."

"So you mean you believe that God has a sense of humor?"

"I'd say he gets enjoyment out of the simplest of things. His love for us is more than my heart can take sometimes. He pours his love into my soul and fills it up so much when I do something good that I almost feel like I'm drowning in pleasure." I looked startled at Colleen and said, "This is all theoretical, of course. Please don't tell anyone."

"Oh, of course I won't."

I continued to eat breakfast, and she saw that I was closing up on the subject.

"So Freddy, do you suppose that you would take time to eat lunch if I packed you one?"

"You bet."

She turned back to the counter and started cutting some roast from last night's dinner. She made me two sandwiches and put in an apple too. "Do you have anything to drink in your lab?"

"Water."

"Good. Water is best for you. When you come out, you'll need to drink milk. I'll make sure we have fresh milk for you. Any chance you're coming out today?"

I thought about it and said, "Not likely."

✦

Gray exclaimed, "God?"

Most everything went black, except I could sense the machinery. I started trying to figure it out.

Green said, "Yes, master. They think they have several gods."

Blue added, "We are checking on this. It has come up in nearly all subjects. We believe that a superior life form is leading these creatures somehow, teaching them, perhaps telepathically. It is a strong being or beings, as it seems to have many names. It may rival us in strength. We have found traces of an unknown substance in several places designed to watch this planet. They do not belong to any creature we have found, and they have been here a long time and just recently used."

Gray looked shocked. "Why were we not informed?"

A voice behind Gray, belonging to nothing I could sense, said, "Because we deemed it not necessary."

All bent over in what had to be the deepest of bows and stayed there. The voice said, "Rise, and get on with it. Blue, you will report to me at the end of this session. Green, you will protect this creature with your life. If anything happens to it, all three of you will answer to my displeasure."

Blue stood up saying, "Yes, Majesty. As you wish, Majesty."

I sensed that the disembodied voice was not there anymore.

Gray let out a telepathic sigh. "I wish I could sense him. It is very unnerving to have him talk only inches from my receptors."

Green said, "He visits here often. We are use to it."

Blue said, "Go slowly, Green. Do not harm the creature."

C H A P T E R 3

✦ ✦ ✦

PARTY TIME

fter breakfast I moved all the supplies inside my workshop and started correcting my design for the shuttle. I came out four nights later, around two in the morning. The watch came out and walked me inside. I cleaned up and went to bed.

The next morning I checked in with Shop to make sure things were coming along well and then told Home I would be outside most of the day, getting some rest and making plans. It was very busy inside my workshop. I had made several robots and attached them into the shop computer for control. I needed some things completed by these new robots before I could go any further.

The idea of making robots was a good one. At first, it was frustratingly slow, but after I created the first three or four, they did the work I would do and did it better. After that, every robot I made sped up the processes. I made the robots adjustable so that they could accomplish a lot of things. My main shop computer is good enough to run about five hundred robots at a time, all doing different tasks. With them receiving orders from her, I can change the orders, and she can stop the work when she recognizes a design problem. She is actually my best work. She can take in anything I say or do and reason out exactly what I need. That programming took me years to develop, but I started it while I was in college. Home was my first attempt at the design, and it could do more than almost any computer in the world. Shop was the next level, and it runs rings around Home. Luckily, there's no animosity between computers, just facts and programming. I thought about making a computer based on an organic brain, but a bad feeling came over me, and I quickly decided that I could do without it.

I spent the rest of the day talking with the lieutenant, making decisions on a new cook, inventing, talking to Becky on the cell phone, and just resting. I was going to go for a swim, but it was getting very cold outside.

The routine of working and resting went on for the next two months. There were breaks for installing a power and scanner system at the radar site and at the navy base. In addition, we installed a power source in one of the helicopters. They've been running it nearly constantly for a month, and the power still reads full.

One day I was sitting at my workbench in the shop, reading a letter from Becky for the umpteenth time. I had been trying to figure out why everyone was so sad. Their emotions were depressing me, and this wasn't like them. Something Becky had written broke through my work tenaciousness and into my consciousness.

> Dear Freddy,
> I miss you, and I hope you will come see me
> soon. At least for Christmas.

"Shop?"
"Yes, Freddy?"

"What date is it?"

"December 10."

I thought about that and realized that I hadn't seen a tree, decorations, or anything. Time to close up shop for a while. I didn't want to miss Christmas. I needed to go shopping, get presents, and see some shows. I sat for a minute longer, thinking out loud. "My family had traditions at Christmas that I think I should continue."

"That sounds good, Freddy. I have enough to keep me working through this time next month. Go have some fun, and get some rest."

"Good idea, Shop, and thanks."

I left the shop and was met by the commander. Susan had received her promotion and was now a lieutenant commander, but protocol, in less than formal circumstances, prescribed that I could call her "Commander" and leave off the "lieutenant" part.

"What's up, Freddy? You were only in there for one day."

"Susan, did you know it's almost Christmas?"

"Yes, I did."

"Do we have a tree and decorations?"

"No, we don't."

"What fun is that? How are you keeping morale up?"

"It's not much fun, and, actually, morale is a problem that worries me."

"Don't you believe in God and Jesus?"

"Yes, I do, and so does the rest of the team, each in his or her own way."

"Well, then, we have some planning to do—a tree to buy, decorations, shopping for presents, special foods, and a party to plan. Are we having a New Year's Eve party too?"

"I wasn't sure you'd go for something like that."

I stopped dead in my tracks and looked up at her. "Commander James, how are you going to keep the troops happy if we don't celebrate sometimes? Birthdays, Christmas, and New Year's are the perfect excuses to have some good fun, invite the families, or go see families, and watch movies like *Miracle on 34th Street*. That's one of my favorites. We need to watch friends open presents, bob for apples, make snow angels, string popcorn. There are so many things that we need to do! This isn't a wish or something I just want to do. This is much more important. This is celebrating the birth of Jesus Christ!" I put my hands on my hips and said, "I love Jesus and want to celebrate his birth, so are you going to help or not?"

She smiled really big. "I would be glad to help, but my orders are to keep you working as much as possible."

"Bah, humbug! I'm going to party. Are you with me?"

"You bet!"

"Good, but don't tell anyone yet. Let's get cleaned up, have something to eat, and then during dinner, I'll broach the subject with the others. I'll bet we pull everyone into the fun."

She smiled. "They're worried that because you're a scientist, you don't believe in God, so you wouldn't do anything for Christmas. This will be a big help, Freddy."

"Didn't Colleen tell them what my beliefs are?"

"No. Why? Does she know?"

"Yes, she does, but I asked her to keep it to herself, and she did. I like that I can trust her."

"You can trust all of us, Freddy."

"It's good to know that, because just after the holidays I may need your help in the shop. I need to test some things." I could feel her genuine relief, like drinking from a cool spring on a hot day. I turned back toward the house and secretly smiled.

During dinner I assessed the emotions around the table. Almost to a person, the morale was low. Everyone wanted to address the thought that Christmas was coming soon, but no one said anything. Sometimes orders can be taken a little too literally, and that can be good or bad, depending on the circumstances. I thought about a good way to start the conversation.

"I have a question."

Katie took the bait and asked, "What would that be, Freddy?"

"Why don't we have a Christmas tree?"

That opened up the floodgates, and everything escalated from there. Plans were immediately made for getting a tree, decorations, shopping, bringing in loved ones, sending out gifts to their families, and a special dinner with all the trimmings. A New Year's party was part of the plan, along with, of all things, a Super Bowl party. That was a tradition I'd never had.

Everyone volunteered to handle different parts of the plan, and the commander assigned teams for the big stuff. The master chief was really happy that we were going to celebrate, but she reminded everyone that watches and protection were not to be compromised.

I said to all that the watch on duty for Christmas and the one on New Year's would be specially compensated. "The commander will decide what the compensation will be, and I will pay for it." I turned to the commander and said, "I would be happy to pay for round-trip airline tickets and lodging for them to go home or almost anything else you might suggest."

"Good idea, Freddy."

Shopping was going to be fun, and I suggested that we take a trip to the largest mall in the United States, so we also planned that trip. I called Mrs. Crain, the owner of the local inn and a personal friend, to let her know that I would be coming to town and needed to talk with her to get ideas for presents for her family. She started to give me the old line that I didn't need to do that, but I put a stop to it. I called Betty for the same information, and then I called the mayor.

Miles Devin was happy to hear from me and was even happier when I said I wanted to exchange Christmas presents with the town. We talked about what the town really needed and what I needed. We decided on a new school for the town, but I would only be allowed to supply the materials. He'd call a town meeting and get the rest of them to supply manpower and agree to my request. "Nothing like the raising of a new house, church, or school to bring the town together."

I told him I'd be there at the meeting so that we could make plans.

Everyone was now very busy doing something they loved to do. Their emotions were high, and that was much better than the prevailing attitude of the past couple of weeks. We went into town the next day.

✦

Blue looked thoughtful. "So this superior being sent the creature a mental no on making artificial intelligence."

Everything stayed open. Green said, "Oh no, you don't!" Everything went completely black. Frustrating!

"Yes, sire. It would seem that this being is especially concentrating on this one creature."

Gray said, "Poor thing."

Blue looked at Gray and smiled. "Green, what or who is this Jesus that everyone needs to celebrate his birthday? Did we capture a Jesus?"

Green said, "Just a count"—and then went blank in thought. A couple seconds later, his mind cleared. "The body system says that we have captured eighty-nine of this species with the name Jesus. They say that none of them were anything special that would require mass celebration, though some were in high positions."

Gray said, "Perhaps it is this creature's offspring."

Green said, "No, our records show he was too young at the time in question."

Blue said thoughtfully, "Perhaps it is another name for his God."

Green said, "Possibly. We have counted over three hundred names that it goes by. Nearly this entire species believes in a God and often in the same way. There are many religions that go with this God—Christianity, Islam, Hinduism, and Buddhism, to name a few."

Gray asked, "Why do we know so much about this God and their religions when we know so little about them?"

"They pray."

"What?"

Green said, "When they are in trouble, they talk to their God through prayer. We have allowed this and have learned much by just listening."

Blue ordered, "Gray, find this *God*!"

Gray left for a second and returned. "It will be found, sire. Green, continue."

CHAPTER 4

✦ ✦ ✦

HEARTBREAK

The kids, including Becky, were in school when Mrs. Crain and I sat down at the kitchen table, which was full of pies and cakes for a bake sale, to determine what I could get each of them for Christmas. She gave me several ideas that changed considerably when she found out I was doing the shopping at the Mall of America in Bloomington, Minnesota. She also gave me ideas for the captain and several ideas for her. Once I got her talking about shopping, it was easy to pull the information I needed out of her. I cheated a little and watched her open mind so that I could get her real wants and needs for her and the captain. She did make me agree to keep all the presents down to less than fifty dollars each. I balked at this, but she was very serious that it would make them feel bad if I went overboard. She wanted me to keep it to ten dollars or less, but I talked her into the higher figure.

"The cost of things at the Mall of America will certainly be high, and I would never be able to find anything for just ten dollars." She finally agreed with me. Betty and Janice were the same at not expecting presents, but I finally got them to tell me what they would really like. Betty knew what the mall was like and knew what she could use, so it was no problem, but Janice had no clue. I pulled it out of her mind anyway. I figured that I would be forgiven for using my powers in that way—it was for a good reason.

We ate lunch at Betty's, and after lunch, I sat down with the shop owners and placed orders for the equipment I needed to install my eight new mini-homes—they would be delivered any day now. The construction company and I had agreed on the design, and they had finished manufacturing the buildings two weeks ago. They were coming overland by truck and could be assembled on my property. I was keeping it a secret from the SEAL team. I could barely contain my laughter a few days ago when I heard them complaining about not having enough room. My home has two master bedroom suites and six regular bedrooms. Each has its own bath, but the commander had insisted on keeping the second master bedroom suite and two of the regular bedrooms for guests. That left the one master bedroom suite for me and the four regular bedrooms to be shared by eighteen others. Some stay in tents, but the team had grown, what with cooks, groundskeepers, patrols watching the town, and a constant watch on Becky. I was upset when I found out about that, but the commander informed me that the watch was necessary. They kept the watch very quiet and unobtrusive by using my scanners.

When the kids came home I was sitting at the kitchen table. To my great surprise—and to the surprise of everyone else—Becky wasn't with them. We said our hellos, and hugs were given all around. An hour later, Becky came in the front door, arm in arm with a boy about her age but a little taller. Carroll was the first to see them, and Becky said, "Hi, Carroll, this is Jimmy. We're going steady." I reached out and touched her mind and learned that she liked Jimmy very much, and I was no longer in her thoughts.

Though I was crying deep inside, I hid it and got up from my seat to greet her. Everyone was watching me. I came around the corner with a smile on my face and said, "Hi, Becky! Hi, Jimmy!" I put my hand out to Jimmy and said, "Nice to meet you." That was very hard to do, much harder than developing the faster-than-light (FTL) drive I'd finished last month. I kept my smile and tried very hard to be pleasant, when what I really wanted to do was crawl away and cry. Becky's chin dropped to her neck, and I could see anxiety on her face. No one was saying anything, so I ended the silence. "Aunt Alice"—that was Mrs. Crain—"made cinnamon rolls. She makes the best rolls I've ever tasted. Come on in, Jimmy. I'm sure she has one for any friend of Becky's."

I led the way into the kitchen and motioned for him to sit down, and then I asked Aunt Alice if I could get a cinnamon roll for Jimmy before I left to prepare for that night's meeting.

She said, "Of course you can, sweetheart."

I went to the counter and got him the biggest roll and then got him a glass of milk. I gave Becky a quick hug and said, "It's nice to see you again."

"It's nice to see you too." I could see the tears starting in her eyes.

I waved good-bye to everyone as I cheerfully left the inn. Petty Officer Patricia Henderson was right behind me. I walked through the town, saying nothing, just smiling and waving to people. When we reached the other side of town, I turned into the woods and walked several hundred yards before levitating myself up to the top of a big fallen redwood tree and sat down to have a good cry. After scanning the area, Patricia climbed up and sat down next to me.

"Hurts, doesn't it." It wasn't really a question, just an acknowledgment that she'd been there before.

I looked at her through tears and nodded. "Yes."

She took me in her arms and held me for a while. It took some time, but I calmed down, and the crying stopped. After a while I said, "Becky was my first crush and my first heartbreak. I can't blame her. I'm sure that it's hard for someone her age to be surrounded by boys in school and remain steadfast in a long-distance relationship with a boy. I'm always hidden away and seldom answer her letters. It's not her fault."

"It's not yours either. You have a job to do. Your life has been forced on you through circumstances over which you've had no control. It's going to be very difficult to find someone who can love you for you, who understands your situation and is willing to wait for you. You don't find that kind of love very often and very seldom at your tender age."

I looked up at her and smiled. "It was fun while it lasted, and I have that. I never forget anything, so I will always remember my first crush. I won't look for it again, but I won't turn it down if it comes along. Love is very special." I stood up and turned to her. "I won't let this ruin our Christmas either. We're going to have fun and that's that!"

She stood up and hugged me. "I hope you know that what you did back there with Jimmy was very brave and very kind. I think the whole family is extremely glad that you did not make a scene."

To Patricia's surprise, I levitated us both back down and started back toward town. The big fallen tree was in the way, so I made a motion with my hand, and it flew through the air, landing over a hundred feet away. I didn't even think about what I had done until I heard Patricia's sudden intake of breath behind me. I turned toward her and said, "Whoops! Sorry about that. Guess I wasn't thinking. I'd better be a little more careful."

She knelt down on one knee and took my shoulders

in her hands. "Freddy, how long have you been able to do that?"

"Months now. Why?"

She searched my eyes for a minute. I touched her mind, and she was thinking, "*With that ability, he could crush someone if he got upset. What kept him from harming Jimmy?*"

My eyes widened, and I looked at her with real concern and said, "You're thinking out loud. With that kind of intense thought and worry, I can't help but hear what you're worried about. I promise you that I never even thought about harming Jimmy. I suppose I could have killed him easily, but I refuse to use any of my abilities to harm anyone. I refuse to even think of doing such a vile thing. Please don't think such things about me."

"Freddy, you're the kindest and most gentle person I've ever met in my entire life. I love you with all my heart, and I think the world of you. You are one of a kind, and I hope you never change. I don't know anyone else with your kind of power who would be so good at heart, so kind, so gentle, so loving of people that he always put others first."

"It's the biggest reason I need you, Patricia. It's one reason I'm allowing the team to stay. People can easily take advantage of me. They could control me, using that knowledge. You girls don't do that. You protect me from being manipulated. I love you too."

We hugged and started crying again, but this time it was both of us. When we calmed down, we were way too serious. I needed to lighten up the situation, so I said, "Tag! You're it!" and started running. She chased me for a while and finally caught me when I ran out of breath. She was really quick and would have caught me sooner, but I'm small and can turn faster. We collapsed on the ground, laughing and tickling each other. Soon, we just lay there.

"Time to get up and reenter the rat race," she said.

"Rat race?"

"It's just a phrase people use for the human race, Freddy."

"It fits."

✦

"He threw a tree that was wider than him a good distance away?"

Everything went black. At least, that was what I let them think.

Green said, "Yes, sire. I received the impression that it had to be at least one-quarter of a click long and twice the height of the creature wide."

"Are trees lightweight?"

"No, sire. The tree had to weigh eighty to one hundred cubes."

Blue looked down and started thinking. There was a frown on that face, with eyebrows pulled in like a puppy dog whose master just fell, and it screamed he was very worried. "Green, take a break for a few seconds." Blue left, and in minutes he returned. Walking along with him were two Yellows, which were smaller than the Green, with heads oversized as compared to the others. Gray and Green backed up in fear.

Both Yellows said in a single, high-pinched, telepathic voice that was blended and hypnotic, "This is the creature you tell us about? The one that mentally battles the Green and picks up and throws with his mind these things called trees that weigh eighty or more cubes?"

The Blue bowed and answered, "Yes, Truth Taker."

"We will watch and protect. And we will report your willingness to have us present." They turned to Gray. "Why do you back up? What are you hiding?" They turned in unison to Green, "Do not wait on us."

✦ ✦ ✦

BREAKTHROUGH

Patricia smiled, and we headed back in a very good mood. When we came out of the forest, people were looking for us. The commander was headed our way, using a scanner to find us. Her head was down as she looked at the readings.

"What's up, Commander?" I asked as we emerged.

She jumped back only a few inches, but it was the first time I had ever seen her startled. I could not help thinking, *She really needs to learn how to use the scanner better. She should have realized we were right in front of her.*

"Freddy! Petty Officer Henderson! Where have you been? Carroll came to us saying that you might need help."

I said, "It was very nice of her to be concerned. I'll have to remember to thank her. Commander, I did need someone to talk to, and Patricia was there to help. We worked things out, so there's no real problem."

The commander smiled at Patricia. "Very well. You had us worried because you two were gone a long time. Where do you want to eat dinner?"

Patricia said, "Let's eat at the diner tonight. Does that sound good, Freddy?"

"I think that would be great. I'll go on ahead with the rest of the team. You hang back with the Commander, Patricia. Judging by the look on her face, she wants you to give her a report about this. You know how she hates to be left in the dark."

Patricia nearly broke out laughing, as we had talked about that very thing while walking out of the forest. "I think you're right," she said.

I headed off toward the diner, holding Colleen's hand on the way. I still needed a little comfort, and Colleen was the closest person to a mommy that I had, besides the commander. About halfway there I heard the commander exclaim, "He *what*? I want to see it before it gets too dark." They took off at a run, back toward the forest.

I looked up at Colleen and slowly shook my head. "Sometimes the commander has no patience. Nope, none at all."

"Freddy, I have the feeling that you're going to teach her patience or give her a heart attack. After taking care of you, I think she'll do real well with kids of her own."

"I'll try my best." I said with a sly smile that screamed *"Just wait and see!"*

Dinner was great. I was starting to see the difference between great food and supposedly great food. The new chef at home was a five-star, and she made things like I do—way too fancy sometimes. She had strange taste, and she never used the right spices. Last week we had an Italian dinner, and I don't think the garlic bread even had garlic on it. So Colleen went back to doing the cooking while the commander looked for a replacement, someone a little more down-to-earth. Everyone was happy about that.

During dinner I asked, "Does anyone on the team like to play video games?"

Leaning forward with interest, Katie answered, "Most of us like to play video games of all kinds. Why?"

"I may have a challenging one for you, and I just wondered if you'd be interested. It's very important that you become proficient with it."

Everyone was looking at me. Katie tried to touch my mind, so I mentally pathed to her, *"Where are your manners?"* She stopped right away. "Freddy, if you made a game for us to play, I'm sure we will all be very interested. I don't believe it's fair that you would bring this up and then not tell us a little something about it."

"When we get back to the base, I'll show you and answer your questions." I looked around and saw media people talking quickly into recorders. One was taking pictures but trying to be discreet. "I don't think this is a very good place to talk about it. I just needed to know for some planning that I'm doing, and I had forgotten to ask that question. I'm glad you like playing them. Who's the best?"

That started some discussions, and they continued with it, even after Patricia and the commander returned. The commander had a strange look on her face.

"I stepped over the line, didn't I?" I asked.

"Yes, Freddy, you did. I have to report it, but I can also report your attitude about the use of it. That should make it all right. I doubt that they will worry if they know that you use it only to help build things."

"If I gave you something more, a tiny breakthrough to report, would that make any difference?"

"It might."

I wrote on a piece of paper. "Susan, let the president know that I have developed a way to travel faster than the speed of light without any danger of crushing the pilot. I plan on testing it soon. Starting tomorrow, I'm going to be training some of your team to help fly the prototype, if that's okay with you."

"Freddy," she said with a smile, "you call this a *tiny* breakthrough?"

"Do you want to discuss some bigger breakthroughs here?" I asked, using my eyes and a tilt of my head to point out the media.

"No!" She took the piece of paper, went outside, and burned it. Then she used her foot to rub the ashes into the dirt. No one seemed to be watching her, and everyone was acting like nothing was happening, but you couldn't cut the emotions and curiosity with one of those knives the master chief was carrying, hidden somewhere.

Dinner went well, and the discussion turned back to who was the champion at video games. It seemed that some were good at driving, some at flying, some at shooting, and some at handling multitasking situations, but all were very good. This was going to work out better than I'd thought.

✦

The two Yellows said, "So he is the one that invented their FTL drive. Amazing."

Everything went blank, except what I was concentrating on. The Yellows walked over to the tank and placed a tentacle into my head. In their dual voice, they said, "He is getting free, child of Green. He is trying to use telekinesis to turn the power off to this tank. You were correct, Blue; you need us. Green could never see this."

Everything went completely black. I could not even think.

"We will keep him under control while Green abstracts the information. Green is far more delicate in these matters than we. Back to the FTL drive—we are assuming this is their first faster-than-light drive."

Green looked astounded that Yellows were being helpful. "Yes, Truth Taker, this is their first."

Yellows said, "We would like any information you gain on those drives. They are faster than ours."

Gray looked shocked. "I do not think that their insignificant drives are faster than ours."

Yellows turned and said in an accusatory tone, "Then please explain why, when you ordered retreat, they gave chase and have already caught and destroyed seven of our ships!"

Gray would have turned pale gray if he wasn't already. He exclaimed as he ran out, "No one tells me anything!"

Yellows said, "There will be a new Gray in his place shortly."

Blue looked sad. "Just when we had him trained to keep quiet."

Yellows said, "That Gray retreated and lost four ships in the maneuver and now seven more ships. He is leading their fleet to our home world. He has gained Black's attention."

✦ ✦ ✦

CHAPTER 6

SURPRISE CHRISTMAS REQUEST

After dinner we went to the courthouse for the town meeting. Devin Miles, mayor and owner of the hardware store, was calling the meeting to order when we arrived. Media was set up in the back. I sat up on the platform where the judge normally sits, except they removed the big podium and replaced it with several chairs. Mayor Miles motioned for silence. "Dr. Anderson has a request that I think would be beneficial to us all. Dr. Anderson?" He motioned for me to take the stand.

"Hi, everyone, it's nice to see you again. Where I live, I have a dock for a boat. I would love for some of you to visit me. Just give me a heads-up so you don't spook SEAL team!"

Someone in the back yelled out, "And get our butts kicked."

I smiled. "That too. My friends have used the helicopter to bring in food and supplies, and that can be expensive and loud. If we had a dock in town, then we could use boats to travel back and forth. The problem is that the only place to put a dock without having to do any dredging is right in front of the schoolhouse, where that old broken-down dock is. I was talking with the mayor recently and learned that the town has size and comfort issues with the present old schoolhouse and would like to replace it. I don't wish to interfere with the existing school while construction is going on, so I would like to propose that we build a new school up the shore just a little ways, and then I could have a new dock built for the team to use after the new school is finished. I would be more than happy to help with the design of a larger, better school and would pay for all of the materials. Mr. Miles said that you might be willing to supply the labor. This would give us a new dock for our use and give the town a new school with all of the most modern amenities. If we started ordering construction supplies now, we could have everything ready by spring."

Several people stood up and started talking.

The mayor quieted them down and gave the floor to a woman I'd never seen before. She was young and had a kind look about her.

"Dr. Anderson, I am Mrs. April Medvinsky. I teach at the 'old' school, and you're so right. This town's schoolhouse is in deplorable condition. It's much too chilly in the winter for the children to concentrate on their studies, and it's long past time we separated the lower classes from the upper classes. I would like to be included in the planning of a new school. Can we have multiple classrooms and more teachers? Can we have computers and new textbooks? What does your generous gesture of kindness encompass?"

I looked at Devin and then back at her. "Mrs. Medvinsky, I'm not the person you should be asking. The planning of this school, if the town approves it, is up to the townspeople. I am willing to put up ten million dollars for construction materials. If that amount is to include computers and new textbooks, the townspeople can vote on that. Right now, we haven't even determined if my request is a possibility."

The entire room was talking again, and Mayor Miles had to quiet them down. The talk was about the amount. They seemed to think the amount was more than generous. Devin pointed to Mrs. Medvinsky and said, "April, if we agree on this resolution for Dr. Anderson's proposed project, then I am sure no one will complain about your being on the school-planning committee. Mr. Marks, you have a question?"

"Yes, Mr. Mayor. I have a great interest in this school, as I have seven kids freezing in it now. My question is why? Why are you doing this, Dr. Anderson? You could buy up land, and dredge it, and put in a small pier anywhere along here at considerably less cost. Why are you willing to pay such a large amount of money to move the school a few hundred feet?"

With a smile, I addressed Mr. Marks. "You don't believe in a free lunch, do you? Neither do I. In all truth, I need this town." I paused for effect. "I need the help of everyone in this town. I cannot complete my projects without help, and I would rather have help from the people of this town than other possible considerations." I paused again to let that settle in. "It just so happens that I have come to love some of the people here. Many have shown me kindness that I have never known before. I'm sorry … I get kind of emotional talking about this, so please forgive me if it shows. In my somewhat short life, I have been taught that if you treat everyone with kindness and honesty, then they will treat you likewise. If someone treats you with kindness and honesty, then you should do two things for that person: treat him the same, and do things that will make him want to continue to work with you. Can you understand that?"

"Yes. That's a good way to do business and go through life, but that doesn't answer my question."

I thought for a minute. "Here's your answer." I raised

my hand as he was about to say something else. "Please let me finish ... When interacting with this town, my plan is to make sure that each interaction is mutually beneficial. I've already stated my reasons why I want to do this. Also, I do not base my reasoning on short-term financial considerations. Sure, it may cost me in the short term, but my primary consideration is what the long-term cost will be versus the long-term benefits. You should be aware that I base most of my decisions on actions and reactions. I look at what the reaction is likely to be and whether that reaction will help or hinder the achievement of my goals and the completion of my projects. I am not trying to manipulate you or the people of this town. If I were, I certainly would not be so candid about my plans. It's true that I can afford to buy the land for a helicopter pad and have it fly in here two, four, six, or more times a day to pick up the supplies that I need, but that would disturb the tranquility of the town, which would not be beneficial at all. The reaction? Some people would be upset that I'm constantly flying a helicopter over their homes, so I won't do it.

"I could easily afford to buy beachfront property and dredge a harbor so that a fairly large boat or a small ship could dock here. That would add a marina to the town, but it would ruin the fishing south of here and possibly harm the environment and sea life by changing the currents. The reaction? Captain Crain, a man I very much like and respect, would be very upset and so would a lot of others whose livelihood depends on the fishing industry. This would not be beneficial for the town either, so I won't do it.

"I could build a road into my land and devise a way to get the equipment or visitors up and down the cliff, but this would not benefit me, as I want to keep the media as far away from my property as I can, and a road would help them to reach me. Or I could use the natural channel where the old pier is located. As it stands, the old pier is useless and dangerous to everyone because it's falling apart. A new pier would have to be built in its place, and that would be beneficial to the town and to me. The reaction? The town gets rid of an eyesore and receives a new pier that is safe for everyone's use, and I have a more convenient, environmentally friendly means of bringing in supplies, so everyone is happy.

"There's a problem with that plan, though. The old pier is right next to the school. The trucks using the road to load or offload supplies and equipment would constantly interfere with the school's activities, and that would not be beneficial. The reaction? The teacher could not teach, students could not concentrate on their lessons, and the parents of school-aged children would be unhappy because their children would not receive a proper education, so I cannot build a new pier unless the school is moved.

"You must admit that the present school building is in a serious state of disrepair. Moving it would be costly and, more likely than not, it would fall apart during the attempt to move it. So moving the school is not a viable option. Building a new school is an option. The town needs one, and I need the land that the old school is sitting on to build a new marina. Building a new school is mutually beneficial, as I get the pier I need, and the town gets a new school *and* a new pier.

"The cost in the short run is very high, but let's look at the cost in the long run. When I add up the cost of using a helicopter for the next five years versus the cost and ease of using electric boats, I will realize a huge savings. First, I am presently borrowing a helicopter from the navy, but I will eventually need to buy my own. The transporting of equipment, personnel, visitors, materials for my projects, groceries and other supplies, and the changing of the watch for the SEAL team will naturally increase over the next few years. We're talking about a large amount of coming and going between my home and the town and a cost in the tens of millions.

"Second, I would prefer to buy and use boats that run on electricity because they are cheaper and quieter to operate and because they won't pollute the environment.

"Third, the goodwill of this town is very important to me. I want to help my friends, like little Annabelle Crain, so that they don't have to try to learn in a freezing classroom. And generally, doing good deeds goes a long way to lowering long-term costs and building community trust. I need your support and protection." I spread my arms wide to show that I meant all of them. "You've made me a part of this town. And this"—I gestured to the commander and her team—"is my family. I intend to keep that trust and love by sharing my God-given gifts with my family and with you … if you are kind enough to let me."

There was a standing ovation. I shrank back as if I were being attacked. They rose to their feet so quickly that it startled me. The commander was immediately at my side, calming me down. I don't know why I was so jumpy. I just was. I returned to the stand, and the mayor quieted everyone down again. I finished by saying, "Mr. Marks, I appreciate your question. I would have asked the same thing. I hope my answer was good enough."

"I'm not sure I believe it, but it sure sounds good, Dr. Anderson."

"Thank you, sir." I looked out over the audience and asked, "Any more questions?"

Someone in the back yelled, "Let's vote."

There was a large amount of laughter and affirmations to that statement, so the mayor got up and raised his hand for quiet. "Before we take a vote, are there any more questions?"

Total silence. Then a hand went up at the right front. Devin didn't seem to see the old woman, so I pointed to her. "Mr. Miles, there's a woman right there with her hand up."

Devin looked where I was pointing but still didn't see her. She smiled and looked up at me. Her hand was still up. I said, "Devin, she's sitting right by that small table, and there's a young lady with her—you can't miss them." The people in the area where I was pointing stepped back.

The commander came up and asked, "Freddy, what does this woman look like?"

"Can't you see her? She's right there! Mayor Miles!"

Mayor Miles asked, "Describe her Freddy."

"She's short, I think. It's hard to tell because she's sitting down. She's sitting very straight and has long hair in a braid down to about the middle of her back. She's wearing a heavy blue cotton dress with old-fashioned petticoats and a pinafore. It looks like she's been working in the kitchen, because she has flour on her hands and clothes. So does the girl. The girl has a light-green flowered dress with some embroidered lace around the collar. She is also wearing petticoats. She's taller than the older woman and has long blonde hair that hangs down below her waist. She's the spitting image of Carroll Crain. She's very lovely."

There was a little fear and some real wonder in the emotions of the congregation.

The media asked people in the back what was going on.

Devin Miles said, "Ask her what her name is, and repeat what she says … because we can't see or hear her."

I looked up at the commander, and I must have looked shocked as the commander started to rub my back, and she normally only does that to calm me. I looked at the woman and asked, "Please, ma'am, may I ask who you are, and do you have a question?"

In a small voice, she mumbled something that the sweet

young girl repeated in a higher-pitched voice. "Yes, young man, I do. It's more like a request." The girl added, "This is Annabelle Crain, and I am her granddaughter, Pamela Crain."

When I repeated this out loud, the congregation stayed dead silent, but their fear increased to a point that made it hard to breathe. "Go ahead, miss," I said.

The woman stood up on weak knees and muttered something else, and the young girl repeated it. "Dr. Anderson, you have come to this town and have done favor after favor."

I bowed in thanks as I repeated her words.

"You fixed the poisoning of our waters at no cost to the town. That is something that cannot be repaid in their lifetime. You have helped their economy so that they can safely say that all of them can enjoy a good Christmas for the first time in many years. Now you have come up with this excuse—and that's what it is, an excuse—to help them some more by building their children a good school. You are a kind and sweet child."

I repeated everything she said, and by this time, I was blushing deeply. I said, "Thank you, miss."

"My grandmother and I wish to ask another favor of you."

"Go ahead."

"Please, Dr. Anderson, for Christmas we would like a proper burial—in hallowed ground so that we can finally rest."

I must have turned white as a sheet because the commander took my right arm, and the mayor took my left. I never took my eyes off the women. Devin whispered to me, "This is the great-great-great-grandmother of Captain Crain. She has been haunting this town as long as people can remember. Find out where their bodies are."

I asked, "Mrs. Crain, can you show me where your bodies are so that we can fulfill your wish?"

She raised her hand as if to motion me to follow and started to slowly walk outside. I moved down to her side. I could feel her touch, but it was not solid so I could not help her along. We talked about many things regarding the Crain family, and I noticed that Devin was taking notes on everything I repeated. As we walked, she told me about her father, who was also slightly telepathic. The reason that they had moved out here was to be away from everyone else. She told me that there had been a rockslide while she was out with her granddaughter and that they had been trapped in it. Everyone looked and looked, but they were never found.

As we walked into the woods, she related how others started moving into the area and how her husband had started the town with his own bare hands. She talked about how he'd go fishing and sell dried fish to other towns inland, and that was how he made a living as the first fisherman in the area. She smiled a tiny, tired smile when she told me how Mr. Crain didn't even like the taste of fish. I listened and related her words. She talked about Mayor Miles's great-great-grandfather and that he was a deckhand who was as clumsy as they come. "More into trouble than out, but his wife and I were the best of friends. She's proud of her great-grandchildren, especially Devin; you tell him that."

We came to a small canyon with berry bushes covering most of the area. It was very much impassable by human standards. She pointed. "We're right up there, near the middle, right in the V of the gorge. We we're picking berries when the rocks came down. I think there was a bear up there, and he accidentally shifted some rocks. Tell my children that it was a quick death." She turned toward me and patted me on the hand. I could barely feel it.

The young girl said, "Forgive Becky; she's young."

I said, "I already did."

She smiled and pointed to my heart. "You're young too. It will mend."

I started to cry, and suddenly, they were gone. I looked at Devin and asked, "Do you know this place?"

"Yes."

"No chance of being unable to find it if we leave tonight and come back in the daylight?"

"No chance."

"Then let's go back to the courthouse."

We walked back in silence. The captain's wife, Mrs. Crain, was right there with us. I don't know when she showed up, but I'll bet it wasn't long after leaving the town proper.

In the courthouse, I sat down and waited for silence. There was a lot of talk, but none of it was "he's nuts" or "cuckoo" or anything like that. Several people were in the back, explaining everything to the media. Everyone was concerned only with exhuming the remains and burying them in a proper resting place. Things were yelled back and forth. "That's a big area, and it could take months, and the rain and snow could stop us long before we get started."

"Yeah, it's a big project, but it's got to be done!" yelled someone else.

"We need to put everything aside and start right now if we expect to have even a small chance of getting it done by Christmas," said another.

Devin had been filling in Mrs. Crain on exactly what had happened and what they found out. She stood up, and it quickly became very quiet. Mrs. Crain said, "My entire family will be out there tomorrow. The inn is closed until I can fulfill my husband's ancestors' request. I'll take all the help I can get. We'll need it."

I put my hand on her shoulder and stopped her. "I'll be going back home tonight." Before she could ask why, I put my hand in hers. "I'll be back with flyers, scanners, and other equipment I have that can locate and remove Annabelle's and Pamela's bodies from that place. The SEALs and I will do this with help from the good Dr. Jenson. She'll need to identify their bones." I looked at the doctor, and she nodded her head. "They will not want to be mixed up. You can come or send others as you wish, but it will be dangerous, given the way the rocks are up there, so don't bring any little ones. Someone needs to stay behind and prepare proper resting places for them, select caskets, and plan a memorial service. The recovery effort will not take long. Commander, what's the weather report for the next two days?"

"We're not looking at snow until Saturday."

"Good. That gives us two days to get them out and one day for the ceremonies. Mrs. Crain, when is the captain due back?"

"The day after tomorrow."

"Good. He'll be able to preside over the ceremonies. I think he needs to be here. You radio him, and let him know. Commander, we have work to do. I want to be back here first thing tomorrow. Let's go."

I started to leave, but Mrs. Crain took me in her arms and hugged me, saying, "Thank you."

She was crying, and I hugged her back. "That's what friends are for, Mrs. Crain." She kissed my forehead and let me go.

When we were in the helicopter, I looked at the commander and said, "Now, that was scary."

She smiled and said, "Yes, it was." She thought for a second, and then, with an abrupt change of subject, said, "Freddy, the project you're working on is God's project, isn't it?"

I looked at her and said very seriously, "Let's not go there. I don't need the president thinking I'm nuts."

"This is off the books, Freddy. I need to know. I have my reasons."

I looked at her quizzically and asked, "May I read them?" She whispered, "Yes."

I reached up and touched her head, letting her know that the world was coming to an end and that I was trying to stop it. I did not let her know why or how. In exchange, she let me know why this knowledge was important to her. When I let go, I put my arms around her and stayed that way until we were home. She's Christian, and her love for God and Jesus are very strong, and now she knows why I'm so driven.

All she said was, "You're not alone, Freddy. I—no, *we*—will help you. We won't let the human race die. You have my word on that."

✦

Yellows asked, "Have you reported this pending disaster?"

Everything started to go black, but I fought it and kept a way to see.

Blue answered, "Yes, Truth Taker. However, we believe that the creature has already taken care of the problem. That is why we could not detect the issue."

"Yes, this is possible. Did you note he can see into the ethereal?"

A wicked look crossed Blue's face. "Yes, he would be able to see our sovereigns if we allowed him his abilities."

"Yes, he would. Do not report this to anyone, especially Gray."

"As you wish, Truth Taker."

Yellows turned to Green. "Please continue."

CHAPTER 7

✦ ✦ ✦

DIGGING UP
THE DEAD

The next day we took off with all the equipment we would need aboard two new-style flyers. It was hard, trying to fly around on a skid with just six disks for control, so I made two large boat-style flyers like I'd seen in cartoons. The controls were easy, but I tried to make them look a little less "juvenile" this time. Every SEAL except two were with us. Katie was one of the two who stayed behind. Being telepathic, she didn't want to meet our friendly ghosts.

We reached town at about a quarter after seven in the morning and picked up the mayor. He showed us exactly where the canyon was and watched with interest while we used our scanning equipment.

The media was there in helicopters but stayed away. Susan talked to them and let them know that the pressure from their props could cause an avalanche, and they moved back a little further. They were being very nice. Susan had also shown me several newspapers that morning with photographs of me walking with the dead. The articles told the exact truth of what happened. I was very happy, so I waved and smiled to the media.

There were a lot of bones in the canyon, mostly those of small animals. I set the scanners to look for calcium, and they found quite a bit. It was easy to pick out the twisted forms of two humans. Their bodies were not that far down, and I used the tractor beam on its lowest setting to lift off one layer at a time. We placed the layers gently down the slope, only a few yards away from the dig. I could have sent them miles away, but I did not want to take the chance of tossing out one of the human bones by accident. It took all day to get to the buried bodies, and now it was getting dark. Not everything could be done with my equipment, at least not without causing more rocks to fall. The sides of the dig had to be shored up and braced while I watched to pull people out of harm's way. Twice we had problems with rocks sliding down, and twice I had to pull people back to the skids. We covered the ground with a tarp, anchored it, and then went home. When we dropped Devin off, I asked him to let the doctor know that we would need her first thing the next morning. We went home, tired and dirty.

The next morning, our prior day's activity was all over the news. Videos showed the SEAL team using the tractor beam, scanning to find the right spot, and people miraculously moved out of harm's way. But it was all positive news about the help the navy, with my assistance, was giving the town.

We headed for town very early. The doctor was waiting for us and so was Captain Crain. "Good morning, Freddy," said Captain Crain as he put his big callused hand out for a shake. "Hope you don't mind, but when I heard that you were digging up my ancestors, I decided to come along for the ride."

The commander answered, "Good morning. Glad to have you aboard. Welcome, Dr. Jenson."

"Call me Karen, please."

The captain helped Karen board my little flyer, and we headed up into the woods, with the media following.

"Say, Freddy, what do you call this skiff?" the captain asked.

"Excuse me, sir?"

"What did you name her? Seems to me that the boat is built to weather land or water. You put sides on her, so she should float if she's not too heavy. You have a definite bow bent back to handle the waves, and the stern is nice and wide. I see tie-downs to moor her to the docks on both sides, and I think I see"—he fingered the rails—"what most of us would call a good line to allow her straight movement through the water. When you were coming down, I saw a V hull with a small pad and four strikes. Put a proper motor in her, and she'd make a nice dinghy—a little larger and wider than most, but the lines are right. You've got to name a boat or ship, boy. It's bad luck not to!" He looked at me with a critical eye and a smile on his face that he was trying to hide.

"Interesting idea, sir. I personally never thought of that. Commander, we need a name for our toys. How about you get the team to name them for me? They can paint the name on when we get back."

The commander said, "Freddy, you need to register them too."

"That creates a dilemma, Commander. Do I go for a license plate, flying numbers, or a boat registration? I won't do it through the state, but if the federal government wants me to number them for identification, then it's not a problem. Can you handle that, Commander?"

"I'll take care of it, Freddy."

"Thanks. Doctor, you doing all right?"

"I'm fine, Freddy, but do me a favor. Keep a steady hand, and keep us closer to land."

Captain Crain laughed. "The doctor gets motion sick, Freddy."

"Sorry, Doctor. I'll bring her down. We're almost there anyway."

When we reached the site, I used telekinesis to lower all of them to the ground, and they uncovered the dig. The captain looked at all the preparations and bracing and said, "There's been a lot of hard, dangerous work going on here."

"We're trying to make it as safe as possible," said the commander. "That's why Freddy is still up in the flyer. He'll pull us out if there's a problem. He has the ability and did so several times yesterday. With him up there, it's very safe. Without him, we'd be weeks just getting here."

"Just between you and me, why is he working so hard on this?" the captain asked. "Why is your team out here helping him? I know it's my ancestors and all, and I'm very grateful—the whole darn town is grateful. My ancestors have been haunting this town for ages, and it tends to scare the holy bejesus out of people, but why is he so interested in getting this done? He's exposing himself and some of his inventions to the media, and I thought he didn't want to do that."

The commander looked back up my way. "Captain, if Freddy says he'll do something, then he will. He is the most tenacious person I have ever known. He told that woman that he would do his best to give them their Christmas wish, and he will. If he had to dig it out all by himself by hand, he would. So if he wants to help dead people today, then today we help dead people. As far as the media goes, everything he is using is patented."

"You people are not at all what I was led to believe."

"What's that, Captain?"

"Trained killers."

She looked at the captain, and, without any hint of

remorse or emotion, said in an even voice, "Yes, we are, Captain. Don't ever forget it. That would be a very bad mistake."

He stopped and watched as she went to the doctor and bent down to help her uncover some of the bones.

After several hours, I yelled down, "Hey, Commander. Would it be helpful if we just take this entire section back to town? I could lift the whole section three feet deep and carry it over to town, if that would give the doctor more time."

The doctor stood up. "Why didn't you say so in the first place?"

"I just thought of it. Sorry, Doctor!"

Everyone climbed back aboard, and I set the tractor beam for a specific area and gently pulled that area away from the site. When we had gained sufficient altitude, I hit the hillside with a blast of energy, causing a rockslide that filled up the digs.

"Don't want anyone falling into that hole."

We took the dig back to town and placed it in the doctor's backyard. She went to work right away, moving bone fragments into two coffins that had been delivered the day before. Captain Crain stayed with her, and we returned home.

✦

"Purple."

Everything went black, except I found a way around Yellows' hold.

"Sire?"

Blue looked thoughtful. "This creature is a mix of everything. He is a great scientist and, therefore, Red. He also contains some Blue—note the helpful and political way he handled the meeting. He has a lot of Purple, in that he does the work. He is a doer. How many Green actually use the things they invent?"

Green thought about that while Yellows answered, "They use their inventions constantly. It is just that many of their inventions are not for scientific research."

Blue smiled. "Exactly. Most are for getting tasks completed quickly and efficiently. Workers use most of the inventions. This creature uses the inventions himself and does not mind getting a little dirty in the doing."

Yellows said, "We see your point. It does seem that most of this species are a mix. Few can afford to be otherwise, with their antiquated monetary system."

Blue continued. "Purple are the most versatile. They work in every place, doing nearly everything, being soldiers, pilots, technicians, builders, and even in this lab, they help out. Without Purple, the elite colors would be lost. This one is an elite Purple."

Green cringed. "There is no such thing as 'an elite Purple,' sire."

Yellows said, "Not so. This is a new species. They are not tested for position at birth. They blindly find their place in their civilization. What if they all started out Purple and worked their way up to the correct color?"

I said, "It's kind of that way."

Yellows quickly clamped down on my thinking.

Green said in revulsion, with a grimace on his face even a mother would hate, "He is learning our language!"

Yellows quieted Green. "As expected."

Green yelled, "Expected! No other has done so in ten thousand years. In known history!"

Yellows set two tentacles on Green and said, "Calm." Green became calm and returned to his scientific clear thought.

Green said, "Blindly finding their place in life would be

complete chaos. How would they know if they chose the correct color? If left to the individuals, they could get it all wrong. Greed and corruption would make some choose the wrong path. And look at the time that would be lost in not knowing what they should do or be."

Yellows said, "Perhaps thousands of years ago, we were the same way. We are wasting time, and he is learning through us. Please continue."

CHAPTER 8

✦ ✦ ✦

THE TRAINER

The next day, after the burial ceremonies, I went to work in my shop. At noon I came out with a mock-up of the shuttle I was building. This shuttle had most of the things in it that the real one would have, except it didn't really work. I had a computer simulator that the shop computer and I had worked on that made it look like everything was fully operational. It was built on a frame that suspended the mock-up between gravity fields so that the unit could move and feel real. Eight generators were concealed inside eight pillars of different heights, which stood out several feet from the shuttle mock-up. The shuttle itself was over thirty feet wide, fifteen feet deep, and fifty feet long. It was smooth and formed like a stingray, with wings that slanted back and were pointed.

I had finished the programming only an hour ago and tested it out. It was connected to the shop computer for lifelike situations. There were sixty planned scenarios, the outcomes of which were completely dependent on the movements and actions of the people running the shuttle. It could be a real thrill ride if you messed up, or it could be as gentle and fun as a walk in the park if you were really good.

I put a protective coating that was nearly impervious to weather on everything so that my trainer would stay shiny. The entrance was through a hatch in the back. As soon as I brought it out, the commander and most of the crew came out to have a look. I went inside the craft to finish setting up the programs. The commander came in, and so did several others.

"Commander, please shut the hatch." She motioned to one of the team, and I heard the hatch close. I turned on the outside speakers and view screens and said into the microphone, "Everyone, stand back. Commander, please take a seat." I motioned for her to take the seat next to mine before I started pointing out the different sections. "That is communications. Please have one of the girls take a seat there." The commander motioned for Petty Officer Henderson to take that spot. "Next is the science officer's spot, which includes sensors, diagnostics, and monitoring equipment." She motioned for Petty Officer Swanson to take that spot. "Right in front of us are the controls for navigation." She motioned for Petty Officer Smith to sit there. "To the left are the weapons and shield controls." Petty Officer Parks sat there. "The rest need to sit down and hold on tight, Commander." They took the extra seats that I had installed for monitoring the exercises. "Ready, Commander?"

"No, but go ahead."

I laughed and said, "Computer, start scenario number one."

"*Confirm scenario number one. Loading. Starting. Home Base Shuttle One, this is Prime Tower. You have clearance to depart for high stationary orbit. Please take off using standard departure vectors.*"

No one did a thing.

"*Home Base Shuttle, please acknowledge my last transmission.*"

I looked back at Petty Officer Henderson. "You're the communications officer. Please acknowledge receipt of that message."

"Yes, Captain." She put on a headset and powered up her equipment. Then she toggled the transmit switch. "This is Shuttle One, acknowledging departure for high stationary orbit."

"Good luck, Shuttle One. You are cleared to go."

I looked down at Petty Officer Smith and said, "Navigator, please take us straight up to a high stationary orbit above home base."

The commander yelled, "Wait!" She turned to me and cautiously asked, "Freddy, are we really going to go into stationary orbit?"

I nearly died laughing. When I finally calmed down, I said, "No, silly. This is that practice game I said I had for you. I won't be finished with the real shuttle for weeks yet."

"Shuttle One, if you don't take off soon, you will lose your launch spot. The next opening is not for three more hours."

"Navigator, take us straight up for five miles and then set stationary orbit."

Petty Officer Henderson looked at the commander and then started working the controls. She was not doing very well, but she finally started moving us up. At one mile, we hit a satellite and crashed.

"Scenario one terminated. Restart when ready."

"Computer, shut simulator down."

"Shutting down."

I stood up with a smile and turned around, asking, "What do you think went wrong, Commander?"

"We were not prepared. We have no idea how to operate this shuttle. This will take time and training."

"That's exactly why I made this mock-up. Do you still want to play?" I got a resounding yes from everyone. "Then let me point out a few things to get you started. Each station has help; just ask the computer to guide you. She will take you through things step-by-step." I turned to Petty Officer Parks. "Always use shields, even if it's just navigation shields. Turn them on. That way, if we hit something, it gets damaged, not us."

I turned to the science officer. "I know that satellite was on your screen. If you see us heading toward something, tell someone. Navigation, always look before you move. You have navigation scanners. Commander, there are sixty scenarios. The last ten are training for my actual plan. When you get to them, I would like to be present for the first two or three. Please have two crews trained, and do cross-training. Everyone needs to know every position in case of an emergency." I opened the hatch and left, saying "good luck" over my shoulder. I watched outside on one of the monitoring screens as the commander asked the computer to access information on scenario sixty.

"I'm sorry, Susan. That information is restricted until both crews have completed all other scenarios."

She hit the chair and cursed. "I'm going to skin that boy alive."

I looked at the girls standing there, watching everything on the screen, and said with a smile, "Whoops, I don't think the commander likes being kept in the dark. I think it's time I go inside and get something to eat." I left quickly, with waves of laughter following behind me. The commander was coming out of the shuttle as I reached the house.

I was sitting at the kitchen table, eating a sandwich, when she came in. She pulled up a chair directly across from me. "Freddy," she said with a gentle voice, like she wanted something. "What are you planning?"

"Gee, Commander," I said with a smile. "Should I tell you before or after you skin me alive?"

"Heard that, did you?"

"Yes. I can feel your emotions, so I know what you're implying. It shows that I'm part of the family when you can get mad at me once in a while. So what's up?"

"You know darn well what's up. What are you planning? Where are you taking us?"

Nearly laughing, I said, "You don't have to go if you don't want to. I can change things around so one person can run it, if needed."

"Freddy, quit playing around. You're making me mad enough to turn you over my knee and give you the spanking you deserve."

I could see she wasn't joking, so I tried to calm down and get serious. "Commander, I told you that I was working on getting to first base, but we have a project before that. What do you think shuttles would be used for?"

"To transfer supplies, to help set up a city on the moon?"

"Exactly. It's dangerous work, and there's a lot of cargo handling in the scenarios, but even before that, I need people who can fly my inventions to fix another small issue first."

"Freddy, can I increase our complement to handle this situation?"

"Of course! Do what you think is necessary, but remember, I get to approve them."

"When we get to the moon, how are you planning to go outside?"

"That's simple. We'll use personal shields. I can easily make shields and utility belts that will supply heat and air, allow dumping of waste, and protect us from radiation. We'll test them in a few weeks. I figure that skin-diving will work for that."

"We won't need those big suits the astronauts use?"

"No way! How can we work if we're wearing that stuff? It'd just get in the way. I am impressed with our astronauts getting anything done in those cumbersome outfits. It must be very difficult."

We sat there for the next five hours, planning out what I could do and what she needed to do. Early on, we were joined by most of the crew. Some were playing with the new toy. They came up with some great ideas. The commander said, "There are experts who have already figured out what needs to go first to a moon base. I'll call them and get ideas on whom to contact."

"Some experts on setting up a base would be great, Commander. But please talk with the president first, and get her thoughts. I don't want to step over that line and upset her."

"Don't worry. I won't let that happen."

✦

Blue asked with some irritation, "Game? His first ship is a game? What is a game?"

Green answered, "A game is not fully understood. At first we thought it was something that children do to pass the time before going to their form of mind-conforming protocol they call school. Then we found out that games are used to teach as entertainment and to bash each other senseless, as with destructive games called football and soccer. At this time we see 'games' as possible military training for the masses. There is almost always a winner and a loser."

Yellows added, "It has come to our attention that they call many games 'war games.' This conforms with many of the messages we witnessed in their transmissions."

Blue said, "Then Gray was correct in thinking that they are trained for war at birth. No wonder they are so devastating."

Twenty Grays marched in and stationed themselves around the room. They were in armor and heavily armed. The large Gray who was leading them looked like he would kill for no reason. He said in a voice meant to intimidate, "Devastating isn't the half of it. Our commanders are now trying to figure out how to keep them from destroying our home world. All but one of their ships passed us and are heading that way. As they passed, they sent a message in every language they know."

Yellows asked, "Was the message deciphered, little Gray?" Their intimidation did not work, as Blue and Yellows were not the least bit afraid.

"Yes."

Yellows decided to do their own intimidation. "Well!"

The Gray backed up a little. "The message was the same three words over and over: 'Give him back.'"

All eyes turned to me. I smiled. It's nice to feel wanted.

Green quickly continued. "Then we have little time."

C H A P T E R 9

✦ ✦ ✦

NEW PEOPLE-AND ONE'S A GOVERNMENT INSPECTOR

The next eight months were a blur, as I spent most of that time in the shop, coming out only to grab something to eat. I received reports about how the government wanted to have more of the scanners and power systems—a lot more—so I released the full patent to them for temporary use in the research of its possibilities. The girls came up with some requests for changes to the layout of the shuttle controls, and I gladly made them. The more I agreed to their suggestions, the more they opened up. One day, I received a request for over twenty changes—silly stuff like backup systems, lights, IFF (Information Friend or Foe), a black box, and—can you believe it?—restrooms, as if I wouldn't have thought of that for the real thing! It grabbed my attention, and I came out.

There were three people near the trainer whom I'd never seen before, but none of the girls were visible. I went back into the shop.

"Shop, please contact Home, and find out where the girls are."

"Freddy, two of the team are now headed toward the door to this shop—the commander and Katie. Two are in the upper forest, one is in the watch room, eight are in the new home complex, two are in the trainer, and the rest are in the house."

"Shop, please hold. It does not sound like there's a problem." Telepathically, I called to Katie.

"Hi, Freddy."

"I came out, and there were people here I do not know."

"I can sense your worry. How sweet. Don't worry; everything's fine. The girls are all doing well. The extra people are from NASA. The commander thought that it would be good to have their opinions on a few things, mostly to ensure we run legal."

"That would be why I got this long list of requests?"

"Correct. Are you coming out?"

"Are you sure it's safe?"

"It's safe; don't worry. We checked them out thoroughly. They didn't like it, and we did turn down three before we agreed to the five we have now, but these guys checked out."

"Okay, then, I'm coming out."

I opened the door and went through. "Hi, Commander. What's up?"

She knelt down to my level and said, "I'm sorry. I should have warned you or at least placed a watch out here to guide you. When Katie said you were outside but ran back in because you were afraid, we knew we'd messed up."

"That's okay, Susan. Stuff happens, and we learn. How long have they been here?"

"Two days. You really need to come out more often. They have questions that I can't begin to answer."

"That's nice. I don't see why I need to answer anything they ask. Have they been approved by the president?"

"Yes, and to be honest, we're a little excited that they're

here. Two are astronauts in training, and one is an astronaut with four flights under his belt."

"And the other two?"

"One is an FAA safety inspector, and the other is an aerospace engineer from MIT. NASA sent them out to help us figure out what's needed to make your equipment legal for flight and to look at standard connections. They would like it if you could connect to the space station and deliver supplies. Though, for some reason, I feel that they don't believe you're actually going to get anything off the ground. The president had to order them to help."

I thought about that for a minute. "That's an interesting situation, but these people are working with the wrong information. This is just a trainer. It does not have the running lights, cargo holds, restrooms, or any of the hundred other options I've worked out." I smiled. "Commander, they have no idea. I'll be right back. Keep this area clear."

I went back into my shop. "Shop, please open the bay doors, and have two shuttles power up."

"*Complying. Doors open. Shuttle One is at 50 percent power and climbing. Shuttle Two is at 28 percent and climbing.*"

"Shop, please contact Shuttle One and Shuttle Two, and have them move out to the first and third launch pads, respectively."

"*Working. Completed.*"

I watched as both shuttles lifted and moved out, pursuant to their preprogramming. They moved through what looked like a solid rock face and out into the compound. I left the shop and stood next to the commander and Katie. Both shuttles moved soundlessly over our heads and out to the launch pads, where they settled down on "multilanders" and powered down. I pathed, "*Shop, place them on A-1 security, and close the bay doors.*"

"*Completed.*"

You could just barely see the shimmer surrounding them from the shields. "Darn," I said. That startled Katie and the commander. "I need to adjust the security shields so they don't show. I couldn't see that in the lights of my shop."

The commander asked, "Freddy, do both of them do what the trainer does?"

I looked at her in amused disgust. "Commander, the trainer is just a simple device. These two do much, much more." With a smile and a lilt in my voice, I said, "I'm hungry. Any chance the kitchen's open?"

"For you, Freddy, there's bread pudding."

I eagerly started toward home. "Really? I love bread pudding."

We entered the house, and I headed upstairs, yelling back over my shoulder to the commander, "Susan, I'll be down to eat after I clean up. Then we can talk, if you want."

I took a quick shower, brushed my teeth, and ran a brush through my hair, which was down below my waist now. I really did need to get it trimmed. I dried it using my telekinetic abilities and then braided it. I put on some new earrings I'd received from the town for Christmas. I liked these earrings. They dangled nicely and tickled my neck, and the girls had stopped laughing long ago.

Almost everyone was outside around the two shuttles. The commander and one man were waiting for me. They were talking at the bottom of the stairs when I came out. The commander said. "Freddy, this is Dr. Michael Landers. He's an aerospace scientist from NASA and MIT."

I put my hand out, asking, "Are you the same Dr. M. K. Landers who wrote *Space and the Reasons Man Must Conquer It* and *Traveling Faster than Light*?"

He shook my hand. "Why, yes, I am. Have you read my books?"

"Of course. They were required reading for my doctorate in spatial physics."

"Well, it's very nice to meet you, Dr. Anderson."

"Please call me Freddy. We're not much on titles here."

"And you can call me Mike."

"Thanks. Have you had lunch, Mike?"

"Yes. We just ate an hour ago."

"I have not eaten for …" I looked at the commander.

"Three days."

"Thank you, Commander. Three days. I'm a little hungry at the moment. If you don't mind, I have a few things to discuss with the commander, and then can we talk while I eat."

"Of course. Do I need to leave?"

"No, sir. Commander, how's the training going?"

We talked through the meal, and she brought me up-to-date on what had happened in the last few weeks. She stopped long enough to explain to Dr. Landers that I paid little attention to my surroundings when I was working. He laughed and said that his wife often said the same thing about him.

"In essence," the commander said, "the training went well until the scenario of going past the moon and out to Mars. None of the girls has had the training needed to work out the math. Every time they tried, they missed Mars by hundreds of thousands of miles. I asked NASA for help. They sent two astronavigators to teach us, Lieutenant Cal Bergman and Lieutenant Yuan Nguyen. With their help, the girls are at scenario forty-eight." Her eyebrows rose a little when she pointed out the fact that they had crashed or died in one way or another over a hundred times before getting through scenario twenty-six. She said, "That's a ridiculous scenario. Nothing like that will ever happen because there's no such thing as a UFO."

"Susan, did I give you the scanning equipment to watch the solar system yet?"

She looked wide-eyed and startled, took a small step back, and said, "No."

"Remind me to give it to you. You'd be surprised the education it can provide." I changed the subject. "Mike, you had some questions for me?"

"Yes, well …" He paused and then said, "You have just increased the questions I have by a factor of ten."

I smiled. "Then we'd better get to them before I go back to work."

"First, can your craft really do what the scenarios show? Can they really go that fast?"

"You're as bad as the commander here. The trainer is just a simple mock-up of the real thing. Please understand that I was in a hurry when I made the trainer, and I slowed it down to allow the trainees a chance to learn to control it. The two shuttles out there on the launch pads are much faster and have much more capability."

"The two shuttles look like they're able to carry a lot of cargo."

"I built the shuttles so that they can connect to a number of different cargo or personnel carriers. I did not wish to limit myself to having a ship that could do only one thing. I thought about it for some time and decided to use our trucking system as a good way to move materials from one place to another. Our semitrucks can carry any type of cargo, pull a bus of people around, move frozen products through the desert, or pull a house across country. What you see out there are two semitrucks with standard trailers. I can easily interchange the trailers. The reason for the two long wings going down both sides of the truck—or in this case, the shuttle—is that at the end of each wing is a small tractor beam to hold the cargo in place and take some of the weight off the connection. That way, I can use a long trailer without having the end weight pull the truck apart. So to answer your question, these two shuttles can carry anything that we can attach to the rear docking connection and that will fit between the two wings. Once in space, you could connect multiples. So this request to have my connection changed to a standard connection is not needed. If I need to dock with the space station, then I would simply ensure that the trailer has that type of connection on the other end. The connections that you use for the space station are not strong enough for my purposes. I can entertain changing them if the need arises but not on these two; the material I used to form them will not permit changes."

"What do you mean?"

"The material is new, something that I still need to patent, so I won't go into detail, but you cannot cut, drill, scrape, scratch, or mar that hull, not with a laser, a diamond drill, or even other equipment I have that we won't talk about yet. I can dissolve the hull under certain precise conditions and reuse the material, but that would mean scrapping the entire hull. The hull was formed around the connection, so removing it would be impossible at this time. I could try to change the molecular structure by ..."

I got up and walked off, talking to myself. I was thinking about ways to change out the connections when the commander must have taken my face in both hands and turned me around. Her face was only inches from mine when she yelled, *"Freddy!"* This brought me back to my surroundings.

"Are you with us again?" she asked.

"Yes. What do you want?"

"You have a guest, and it's not polite to drift off right now." She turned to Dr. Landers. "See what I mean by 'drifty'?"

I turned red and went back to sit down.

Mike said, "Your amount of total concentration could be dangerous in space or on the moon, Freddy."

The commander added, "Or here. He has walked off the terraces twice, and once he fell into the water. We've had to ensure he has someone with him at all times when he's outside of his shop. I worry a lot about him being in his shop alone."

I turned even redder. The master chief came in and said with a laugh, "He'll break his neck some day and won't even realize it until someone sees his head flopping around."

Everyone laughed except me.

"Dr. Landers," I said, "this is Master Chief Jacquelyn Uniceson."

"We've met, Freddy. After all, I've been here for two days."

The rest of the team was coming in, and the commander made introductions. She was right; it was a good group.

"Freddy, this is Captain Mark Twain Williams. He's the astronaut with all the experience I was telling you about."

"Nice to have you visit, Captain."

"I'm hoping for more than a visit."

I tilted my head, looking concerned.

The commander asked, "What's wrong, Freddy?"

I directed my comments to the NASA captain. "Please understand that I am highly empathic." I paused for this to sink in. "I cannot help but feel what you're feeling, so I know that this"—I held both braids and flipped one earring up about an inch to show that I was talking about my choice of adornment, and I squinted my eyes in distaste—"disturbs you very much."

"Well, sir, I'm just not used to it."

"Be that as it may, please understand that I'm not likely to change. If you wish to remain at my residence or work with me for any length of time, please get used to seeing things that you may not understand or approve. I am open-minded enough to discuss this or any other issue with you, but I cannot and will not put up with someone feeling disgust toward me or any member of my team because of what I consider to be that person's close-mindedness."

"I will try my best."

I smiled. "I can ask for no more."

The commander quickly introduced me to the next two people. "Freddy, this is Lieutenant Cal Bergman and Lieutenant Yuan Nguyen. They are the two astronaut trainees in astronavigation and piloting that I told you about."

Cal Bergman said, "Nice to finally meet you, Dr. Anderson." I shook hands with both of them. "We both are also hoping to be able to do more than just train."

I responded, "It's nice to see two people who have such positive feelings. I can see that we will get along very well."

"Thank you, sir."

✦

Gray asked, "What is a UFO?"

Green quickly turned to laughter inside. "A UFO, master, is an unidentified flying object."

Gray looked disturbed, his head tilted and his face wrinkled. "And what is an unidentified flying object."

Green smiled. "No one knows. That is why it is unidentified."

Every Green in the room laughed inside.

Gray's eyes seemed to wander in two different directions with a look of confusion, so Yellows helped. "Nice joke, Green. OPR, Master Gray. In their language, we were OPR. It seems that anything in space or flying through their territory that they cannot explain is opwernekul (or unidentified), prfereret (or flying), and a ratemer (or object); therefore, UFO. Their language has surprisingly similar words to ours. It is one of the reasons that this creature is mastering our phonetics so quickly."

Gray exclaimed with narrowing eyes, "It is learning our language?"

I decided to mess with them a little more. "*He!* He is learning your language. I am not an *it*."

Eyes widened, and everyone, except the Yellows and Green, backed up as they all looked shocked. Yellows quickly added a third and fourth tentacle, nearly completely covering my head. "We are running out of time in more way than one. He is adapting to the tank. Continue—and hope he does not do anything stupid."

✦ ✦ ✦

INSPECTORS OR PLANTS-PICK ONE; THEY BOTH SUCK

"Freddy," said the commander, "this is the FAA inspector, Mr. Terry Fly."

"Hello, Mr. Fly. I take it you're the one who generated all the change requests? I am very sorry that they started you out looking at just the trainer; that was my fault. I failed to communicate to the team what the real product would be like. I've brought the shuttles out for you to inspect."

"I've already looked at the exteriors. I can see there's a large difference, and many of my requests were unnecessary. When will I have the chance to inspect the interiors?"

"That's a problem, Mr. Fly. Please don't take offense, but I have yet to hear an explanation regarding why I need inspections or approval from the FAA to fly my shuttles over my own property. I suppose the commander has a good reason, possibly several, but she has yet to sell me on this idea."

"It's the law, sir. All equipment flying through United States airspace must meet certain regulations."

I put my hand on his arm and led him into the living room. I offered him a seat and then sat down across from him. "It's not your presence that I am against, sir. If I allow my ships to be inspected, then I am saying that I will allow this for all my ships, and that could be very dangerous."

"Dangerous? In what way?"

"The regulations by which you must abide are dictated by politicians; even some of the laws are purely political. I know because I've read them. I can see a standard for navigation lights—that's common sense—but there are also laws regarding what type of materials I can use. Mr. Fly, most of the materials I use are not on anyone's list yet. You require that I have toilets and a waste-disposal system that meets specific standard regulations, but my disposal unit completely disintegrates the waste, leaving no residue. Most of your regulations govern planes and helicopters, not spacecraft. Those are just a few of the reasons why most of your regulations and laws do not apply to my ships."

"I understand, Dr. Anderson, but my hands are tied on this."

"I was afraid you'd say that, sir. I will allow you to inspect the craft, and I will make any modifications you suggest that make sense to me. You may have some very good ideas, and I will not turn down the opportunity to have access to your expertise; however, I will not make changes that I deem foolish or unnecessary. I am not going to build my craft to please some politician."

"Even if this means that you will not be permitted to fly the craft?"

"I have every right to do what I wish over my own land. I can fly straight up or underwater. I don't need any FAA regulations to do that. I'll take it out underwater three miles and go up from there, or—if it really becomes necessary—I'll buy an island and set up a base outside of the United States.

I will not break the law. I will simply work my way around it, rather than allow my ships to be cluttered with junk, which would endanger the people in them. Let me be more positive, Mr. Fly. I think we can work with each other on this, but we both need to be open-minded and flexible. If you can explain to me why a regulation exists and how it pertains to my spacecraft, then I will try to accommodate you as much as possible."

Mr. Fly was not happy, but what could he do? He knew I was right.

The commander then introduced me to four new navy additions. She had them stand in a row, like they were at inspection or something. The first one introduced was a seaman apprentice just out of boot camp. Her name was Julie Ann Weatherington. I touched her open mind and realized something was wrong.

"It's nice to meet you, Julie. Exactly what relationship do you have with Admiral Bates?"

"None. Why, none at all." Everyone could see the surprise and the blush on her face.

She lied to me. She lied! I was so upset I turned angry, and that means I went completely unemotional, monotone, and businesslike. "Commander, please remove her from my home this instant."

Two SEALs took hold of either side of her and started to remove her.

"Please—don't. Please," she begged.

"Wait," I said.

"The admiral is my great-grandfather. He has no idea that I'm here. I won't tell him anything. I promise."

I nodded. "I can see that you're now telling the truth. Why are you here, and do you have any hidden agendas?"

"I'm here because I asked for this assignment," she said, "and I have no hidden agendas."

"You're lying. That's twice. Commander, please have her removed."

Susan gestured with her hand, the team took the seaman apprentice away. She was crying.

I looked at the commander and said, "I think we need to revisit the questions we're asking people."

The commander asked, "Freddy, was the navy behind this?"

"No, I received the sense that she was hired by another military agency. It felt like the army."

I checked the open mind of the next person, Yeoman First Class Henry Peters, who was about twenty-five years old and stood about five foot eight or nine. He was not a SEAL but had extensive experience in running remote bases, including the paperwork involved. I detected nothing wrong with him. "Hello, Petty Officer Peters." I put my hand out.

"Hello, Dr. Anderson." He had a good firm shake, "I do not have any hidden agendas. I am here because I was told there might be a chance that I could go into space, which is something I have always wanted to do."

"Henry, that is up to the commander. She runs this base and determines who does and does not work with me on my projects. I just let her know what I'm doing and what I think I may need. She's really good at figuring out the rest. I trust her completely. Welcome aboard."

The next person was Lieutenant Robert Handelson. I looked at him and touched his open mind. I quickly stepped back behind the master chief. Three of the team members were on him in a second. He never moved a muscle, as I had him brain-tied, but his eyes followed me like I was some kind of devil. The master chief asked, "What's up, Freddy?"

"Did you screen this person?"

"Yes. The lie detector gave no adverse indications."

"It should have. He's been hypnotized, but that would not fool my equipment. Bring me that lie detector, please."

The commander went to the office and returned with the lie detector. I used my powers to look inside and saw that someone had tampered with it. "Interesting. Who transferred here first—Seaman Apprentice Weatherington or Lieutenant Handelson?"

"Weatherington transferred in first. Why?"

"She may have messed with this device."

The commander ordered, "Bring her back here, and kill him if he moves."

Everyone moved back even farther than they had already.

I moved to the next new member. "What is your name?" I asked.

Trembling, she said, "I'm Dorothy ... Personnelman third class (PN3) Dorothy Pendelson."

"Interesting. Any relation to Professor Jim Pendelson at MIT?"

"He's my father," she said with a smile.

"Great man. I've read most of his books. May I look deep into your thoughts? I'm sorry, but Lieutenant Handelson has made it necessary."

"My father said you'd want to do that. Yes, you may, and thank you for asking first."

I took a good look. She had an interesting mind, but there was no hidden agenda except to try to talk me into letting her father come for a visit. She was here because her father asked her if she would like to make her dreams come true, and she had said yes. Since childhood, she had wanted to be part of something great, something having to do with space exploration. This was her chance, and she'd be faithful and true. Apparently, her father was very interested in what I was doing and how he and his colleagues could help.

I opened my eyes and smiled at her. "I like you. You're

honest, and I think you'll make a great addition to the team. I have no problem with the professor coming to visit me, as long as I'm made aware of it in advance. I think a great man like your father deserves the courtesy of my being present when he arrives. Don't you?"

"Yes. Thank you."

Seaman Apprentice Weatherington was brought back in.

"I have only one question for you," I said. "Did you tamper with this lie detector?"

"No!"

"Remove her. She's lying again. Commander, apparently she was paid to tamper with this unit so that the next person would not be detected, and then she reconnected the equipment after his interview. I can see how she tampered with it. She's very lucky that I removed the explosives, as otherwise, she and half this building would be missing right now. Now I need to find out why." I stayed way back from him as I looked up at Mr. Handelson and said, "We can do this the easy way or the hard way. Your choice."

He bit down hard on his teeth.

I held out my hand to reveal a tooth. "Looking for this?"

He glared at me.

The commander took the tooth. She glared at the man but directed her comments to me. "Freddy, any chance you might see fit to let us have him? I'd like to have the girls play with him for a few days."

That request scared even me. I put my hand on her arm and said, "After I finish with him, we can talk about it." For just a second I could see fear in his eyes, and then it was gone.

I raised my hand, closed my eyes, and entered his mind. Shortly, I knew all I needed to know. I looked at him and said, "Thank you for the information." I looked at the commander and said, "He's an army spy. He's working for a general in the Pentagon. His name is really Robert Handelson, and his rank is the equivalent of a lieutenant in the navy. Captain, I think the army generals kept everything as near to the same as possible. He was hypnotized only to get past the lie detector. He had a tiny piece of equipment that made it jump up only when he wanted. Home?"

"*Yes, Freddy?*"

"Access memory for the time when Mr. Handelson was being interviewed."

"*Researching. Completed.*"

"Were there any jumps in static or magnetic interference?"

"*There were eighteen spikes in static electricity during the interview. None before or after.*"

"Home, if this or anything like it happens again, please report any anomalies right away. Thank you."

"*Compliance.*"

"Why was he sent here?" asked the master chief.

"His job was to report on what he observed here, undermine the leadership of this command, and attempt to get me involved with other army personnel. Apparently, there is a young girl they think would interest me. Home?"

"*Yes, Freddy?*"

"Please contact the president of the United States."

"*Working.*"

"Freddy, what are you going to do?" asked the commander.

"I'm going to give the president a big headache."

The commander said, "Home?"

"*Yes, Commander?*"

"Cancel that call!"

"*Call canceled.*"

"Thank you."

I raised my eyebrows in question. She looked at me and said, "Freddy, I know you can override that, but you put me in charge. I messed up by letting that unit out of my control. It won't happen again. I can assure you that new personnel will be screened a lot more carefully."

"I expected that, Susan. You're not one to make the same mistake twice, but I'm not calling about you or your ability to run this base. I will correct the unit so that tampering is not possible. It's partly my fault that it happened. It was a test model anyway." I shrugged. "We tested it and found a defect, thanks to the army. I'm calling to chew out the president for letting the army interfere again."

"Freddy, chewing out the president is stepping over the line."

"Is it really?" I said with a little sarcasm. "Don't you think not keeping her promise to me is stepping over my line?"

"Freddy, if you were the president, think how you would feel if you thought that someone like you was running out of control, calling high-ranking people, and being generally mad at her?"

"Interesting. Not too happy, I suppose. So what do you suggest? I can't just let it go."

"You put me in charge, so I'll take care of this. But it has to be me who does it. I can't promise that I can stop the army, but I sure will send an extremely strong message."

I thought about that for a minute, and then I smiled and looked at Mr. Handelson. "Sorry. I tried to make it easy on you by just having you court-martialed, but the commander is right. I did put her in charge of these things." I turned to the commander and said, "Susan, please do me a favor."

"What's that, Freddy?"

"I don't want to know, and I don't think our friends here should know what you do about this situation. I don't want to have nightmares, and I'm sure they don't either."

The man started struggling. She looked at him and said, "We'll keep it quiet, won't we, girls?"

She received several "You bet we will, ma'am"s from the team, and he was taken away.

✦

"Black."

Nothing went black. I could still see right through the tentacles, and during that session, I turned down the knob on the machine that ran the tank. It was very difficult, but it turned.

Green said, "I must agree, sire. This Susan did seem to be more Black than most others we captured. Still, she had a lot of Blue in her and some Yellow, I think. I had not thought to look at them this way."

Yellows said, "Order the others to look at the past memories we have taken and see what they think, if categorized into colors."

Green turned to the other Greens and said, "Do it." Then it turned back to me.

✦ ✦ ✦

SOMETIMES THINGS AFFECT US A LOT

Everything was quiet after that. I headed back into the kitchen to get something to drink. Behind me, I heard Mike asking, "He doesn't stay upset very long, does he?"

Susan took a second to answer. "You have no idea. He's thinking right now, letting it set in, and figuring out the ramifications of what this means. Thank God he trusts us enough to know we'll handle it, but God forgive the army if I can't get them to stop."

I turned around and said sadly, "Susan, I'm tired. I think I need to sleep on this. I can't work right now anyway, as I'm too worried that the evil army people will harm you and me. I can't go into my shop right now. Please, could you keep one of my protectors near me? Mr. Fly, I'm sorry, but I can't let anyone into the shuttles right now. Please be aware that they're locked down tight with orders to self-destruct if anyone breaches the shields, so please stay away."

I walked over to Colleen and took her hand. I looked up at her and said, "I don't want to go to my room alone, but

I'm very tired. Would you please come and stay with me for a while?"

Colleen looked at the commander, and the commander motioned for her to go ahead.

When I reached my bedroom, I said to Colleen, "This scares me, and I really don't want to be left alone right now."

"I understand, Freddy."

I heard the commander downstairs, asking Katie, "Could you read him on that last?"

"I received several impressions, Commander. First, he's really scared. He was not kidding about being worried, and all of a sudden, he's very tired, so I think he's going to do exactly what he said. He's not playing some child's game. You know him better than that. He is really upset about this. I received the strong feeling that he trusts us, but he doesn't trust that someone won't find a way into his shop and gas him or something. He's thinking up ways right now to make his shop more secure against intruders. He's also thinking that going to the stars is a folly because when he gets there, the army will just take it away from him, and he won't be able to"—she stopped and stared at the commander—"save the planet from disaster!"

Betsy, one of the SEAL team, said, "Oh God, save us!"

"Commander, he is really upset," said Katie. "Remember the last time he was like this?"

"Yes. He didn't eat for a week, and he did nothing but sleep. We thought he was trying to kill himself. Then it was weeks before he went back to work, and that was piecemeal. He had to redo everything he'd done for a month."

Katie turned to the others and explained, "When he gets worried, he thinks too much and reads too much into everything. He loses his appetite completely, and he gets paranoid and depressed. He can't work like this because he makes too many mistakes, and that causes him to worry even more. Commander, those ships are set to disintegrate if anything happens to them, and so is the shop. I received that very clearly."

"I need to think this through," said the commander. "Please keep up with the training. He has to be present for scenario number fifty-one, and it's just possible that we can pull him out of it then."

Susan went to her office. I watched her thoughts for a few minutes until I fell asleep. I was so tired.

✦

Gray said, "Weakling."

God! I wished they would stop talking and probe me some more. I was tapping into Yellows' energies, and I turned that knob off. I couldn't do any more while Yellows were not occupied with helping the probe.

Yellows asked, "Weakling?"

Gray said, "He has a mental breakdown over some little problem like a spy. How cute. He belongs in the Purple child pens."

Green said, "How dare you say that about a Red of any species!"

Green was so angry that he let go of me and looked around for something to bash the Gray. Blue saw me falling and panicked. A Yellows' tentacle reached out and gently tapped Green and Blue. They became totally emotionless and immediately stopped. Green turned around and came back to the tank. He placed his tentacles under me again and held me up. I touched the sides three times while falling. Green said in an unemotional tone, "The creature is not harmed."

Yellows touched them again, and emotion returned, but

they were calm. "How can this be? It should be dead. We saw it touch the side."

I said, "Seems to me that Green had a little Gray in him for a minute. Perhaps you are not as different as you think."

"Do not be profane, creature. How is it you are still alive?" Yellows asked.

"I turned the switch off."

Yellows looked over at the switch and turned it up fully. Then they ordered, "We want two more Yellows in here immediately, and have Green guard that switch!"

As two small Yellows entered, Blue and Gray backed up. Green would have backed up, if not for being required to hold me centered in the tank. The new Yellows bowed to the other Yellows, and eyes looked unblinkingly at the other colors in the room. A Purple fainted, and two Greens quickly attended him, glad of something to do.

The new Yellows said, "You wish for help, our pen mate?"

Yellows said, "Yes, our friend. Please hold this creature up, and monitor any attempts from him to use mental abilities. If he tries, do not shut him down or erase memories. Simply block him."

"As you wish, pen mate." Six tentacles entered the tank and wrapped around me, holding me directly and firmly in the center. My mind was held in a firm shield, and everything went black. Darn!

Green removed all his tentacles except the one in my brain. Yellows said, "We are sorry, Green, but your emotions would have destroyed this creature, if not for his deception. We cannot afford any more deceptions or mistakes. Please continue."

CHAPTER 12

✦ ✦ ✦

THE PRESIDENT IS COMING

W hen I woke up four days later, it was because I heard Colleen saying in a soft voice, "Freddy! Wake up, Freddy! The president is coming. She wants to talk with you."

I turned over and covered my head, asking, "Why? What did I do now?"

She smiled. "I see you have a sense of humor again. You know you did nothing wrong. Now let's get you up and into the shower, and then we'll get you dressed." She threw the covers back and lifted me up, noticing how underweight and undernourished I was, and she carried me to the shower.

When she turned it on, I woke up. I have a great hot-water system, but it still starts out very cold—ice-water mountain cold. "Hey!"

"Stop complaining, and get going."

"Yes, Aunt Colleen," I said meekly, while shivering.

I cleaned up and started to get dressed, even though what I really wanted to do was go back to bed. The president was in charge of the army, and she had set them on me again. I just couldn't see them disobeying her. She was the boss, and that made her responsible for what the army did, didn't it? Was she against me for some reason? I'd been good, so why was she coming here?

Since it was the president, I supposed that I should dress up a little. I had a suit and tie that the team bought me for my birthday, or I could just dress in my normal work jumper. I could not think, so I went over to the dresser and found a coin. Heads it's the jumper; tails it's the suit. It hit the carpet and bounced, finally settling on tails. I said out loud, "The suit it is, I guess." Luckily, Colleen had already tied the tie for me, so all I had to do was slip it over my head and collar, turn my collar down, and button the flaps. I liked this suit. It was a dark blue with tiny stripes—I was told they were called pinstripes. It made me look like I was thirteen instead of eleven, and I really liked that. I actually felt better for a minute.

Colleen knocked on the door, startling me. She opened it a crack and asked, "Are you ready yet?"

"Yes. I guess so. How do I look?"

She looked at me critically and then tightened and straightened my tie. With a look that seemed motherly, she said, "You'll do."

"Why is she here?" I asked. "Are you going to stay next to me? I don't want to be alone near her."

She bent down so we were face-to-face. "Don't worry, sweetheart. The team won't let anyone harm you, not even the president. You don't need to worry about her. She's not here to punish anyone. I think she's interested in the shuttles."

I looked at her. "Don't lie. You're better than that, and you know I can tell."

"I wasn't lying."

"Scurrying around the real answer is the same as lying."

"Yes, well, sometimes your abilities are a good thing, and sometimes they're not."

"Tell me about it. Sometimes I hate knowing how others feel." I shivered, remembering the coldness of that Mr. Handelson, and said, "But sometimes it saves my life." Nothing was said for a few moments while I tidied up the bed. "I'm tired, Aunt Colleen. How long do you think this will take?"

She looked at me with concern. "A while, sweetheart. She came a long way just to talk with you, and we've planned a dinner for her. You're the host, so you need to entertain her and keep her occupied."

"I guess I can try," I said, feeling downhearted. We left my room and headed downstairs.

Meanwhile, downstairs in the study, planning was going on. Petty Officer Henderson said, "The president will be here in about ten minutes, Commander."

"Great! Katie, how's Freddy?"

"Colleen has him in the shower. Commander, he's unconsciously broadcasting his thoughts. He can barely stand up he's so tired. His thoughts are fear of the president. He feels that she's responsible for the army's actions and that he might as well give up and die. He doesn't want to face her. God, I hope she doesn't make him angry right now. If his fear turns to anger, I have no idea what he'll do. Don't let him get cornered, or he could come out fighting. He called Colleen 'aunt.' He doesn't realize it, but he thinks of her as his aunt and protector." She smiled. "How cute."

"What?" asked the commander.

"He thinks of you as 'Mommy.' He may not say it out loud, but he does."

"Interesting."

"We're like his sisters. I kind of figured that, but he really feels that way."

"What is he planning to do?"

"Nothing. He's so tired he had to flip a coin just to decide what to wear. He's thinking he's glad Colleen already had his tie tied. He's also thinking about going back to bed."

"Where's Colleen?"

"At the top of the stairs, waiting for him."

The commander said, "Betsy, tell Colleen that Freddy is thinking of going back to sleep." Betsy nearly flew up the stairs. "Katie, I know this is spying, and you don't like doing this to Freddy, but I need to know. What are his immediate needs? What can we do to help him? Is there any clue on how to get him interested in working and living again?"

"First, we need to be ourselves, act natural, joke around, and make light of things. He could use a laugh. Show concern if you feel it. He loves us all very much and will take it well if it's sincere. Do not fake anything! Next—and possibly most important—show that you're protecting him. Make a big show of it. Show that you trust the president but not more than you trust Freddy. He needs to see that your concern for him overrides anything the president wants. He trusts us, but he's feeling very vulnerable right now."

"Showing protection for him is easy. The orders stand that we protect Freddy at all costs, and I repeat—*all* costs. If that means taking out the president, then do it. The other could be tricky. I could warn the president that I need to go against her on some things, but he'd see right through it. Let's just hope something comes up that will fit the situation. I can always explain it to the president later."

Katie said, "He's on his way down."

Betsy entered. "Freddy and Colleen are coming down, Commander."

"You have your orders. I want that helicopter fully

scanned, and I want Freddy to see us scan the president and every person who's with her. What are you waiting for? Scatter!"

The commander stood up and walked out to the front. When she saw Freddy, she almost cried because he looked so tired and pale. He needed to hold on to Colleen just to make it downstairs. His little legs were wobbling like there was no strength left in him. His expression looked drab and listless. His normally bright purple eyes were dark and sunken. Susan's motherly instincts were in overdrive. She bent and straightened his tie when he reached the bottom of the stairs, and she hugged him close to her as tears started to flow.

"It's nice to see you too," I said to the commander.

"It's good to have you back from the dead, sweetheart."

I chuckled a little. "Does this mean I can go back to bed now?"

She held me at arm's length, saying, "No way, young man! You're not leaving me alone to entertain the president all by myself."

"Are you still afraid of her? I don't blame you. I am too."

She took my hand and started walking toward the front door—the helicopter was coming in. "No, dear. I'm not afraid of her at all. I'm just afraid of looking bad in front of her."

"I guess that makes sense," I said. "You respect her and her office, and your career depends on what she thinks about you. That would make anyone nervous. After all, she is your boss. You may think the orders make you independent, but they don't, not if your job is still in her hands."

"Freddy, you've always had this knack of seeing right to the real issues," said Colleen. "You understand that we do need to make her happy." Then, while straightening my tie again, she said in a sterner voice, "You be on your best behavior, young man."

"Don't you think it would take some of the tension away if she accidentally slipped and fell in the water?" I asked. "Can she swim?"

Susan looked at me in shock, but seeing my smile, she realized I was pulling her leg. "Don't even joke about such things."

✦

"They would kill their president to protect this creature."

Everything went black, but if you think that's going to stop me, *think again!*

Yellows said, "Yes, and now you know why their entire fleet is headed toward our home system. Not one ship stayed behind to protect their Earth."

Blue turned to Yellows with great concern. "Their entire fleet! We will destroy them easily. They must know this."

Yellows sadly said, "We are not sure they do. Our last Gray leader was so inept this species was winning. They may think they have a chance. What we learn here may save their planet from our fury and this species from total annihilation. No one has ever attacked our home system. The fleets from all the worlds are converging to the home system. Over one thousand battleships. They will be there in plenty of time, and the Gray will not allow a single survivor. Green, please continue."

✦ ✦ ✦

CHAPTER 13

PRESIDENTIAL VISIT

I tensed up dramatically as I watched the incoming helicopter.

"What's wrong?" asked the commander.

"Someone's with her who can read minds. I feel her trying to sense everyone here and pick out emotions."

"Is she hostile? Is the president in trouble?"

"No, and no," I answered. "The president knows she reads minds. Her ability is rather weak but stronger than Katie's. She doesn't have the ability to control others. She reads and transmits, but that's it. She has good mental shields, but her front mind is open and letting us know that they are not a threat. She knows I'm reading her. She says to say hello. She knows someone here."

With that, I relaxed considerably and brightened up as I started toward the helicopter's landing area. I was still too weak to move quickly and had to support myself on the commander, but my renewed enthusiasm was clear.

The commander and Colleen looked at each other and

smiled. I could tell that Susan thought curiosity could sometimes be a good thing. Then it hit her, and she stopped suddenly and pulled me in her direction. "Can you control people, Freddy?"

"Sure," I answered, still looking at the helicopter. "Why do you think that nasty spy didn't move for a while when we talked? I made him think he was tied up tight, thus keeping him from using his legs and arms."

She put two fingers on my chin and turned my face to her. "I don't recall your ever doing that. Have you?"

"Only with animals that I wanted to get a closer look at, and after I do, I usually reward them. Most of the time, they come back on their own after that. Did you know that most birds have tiny little fluff under their wings, and bears have bad breath? I normally would not do that to a person, but the spy wanted to kill us. He didn't like being found out. Not at all. I personally don't think it's right to control anyone. When I had to do that to him, it really upset me, as it goes against everything I believe." I could feel my lips forming a pout. "I was afraid he'd harm one of my sisters. Did you know that—"

She put a finger to my lips. "You're babbling." She smiled and said, "Freddy, have more faith in our abilities. We're here to protect *you*, not you us."

I smiled meekly. "I know."

The helicopter landed, and several people in black suits climbed out. When they started heading in our direction, eight girls from the team aimed fully automatic rifles at them and yelled, "Halt!" Two of the girls scanned the Secret Service personnel and removed their weapons, which made them very unhappy. Once unarmed, they were set in a group to the side and watched under guard. I recognized the president when she climbed out. She looked well and not a bit scared, but her emotions were exactly the opposite.

The young lady who climbed out next was reassuring the president that she was not in danger. She was about twelve or thirteen, and she was beautiful. She told the president that the reaction she was seeing was for my protection, and the girls surrounding them were thinking only of me. She said she felt no animosity at all. Then she looked at me and said to the president that the strongest emotion she sensed was fear of her, and that was coming from me.

I instantly raised my shields, and her eyes widened. She said, "He's stronger than I am by a large multiple, but he's not trying to read our minds. He is listening, however, to our transmitted thoughts, our emotions, and our spoken words. He knows what I'm saying, even from way over there. *By the way, Freddy, I'm fourteen.*"

"Interesting," said the president. She looked at me and asked the girl, "Melanie, if he's so much stronger than you, how do you know he isn't reading our thoughts?"

She giggled. "He thinks it's immoral. He won't do it unless he's protecting himself or his ..."—she paused and tilted her head—"family. Be careful what you propose. He sees these girls as his family, and he's very protective of them."

The president said nothing more but visibly relaxed. This all happened very quickly as the president disembarked. The next person out was a navy admiral. It seemed like he was covered in gold, especially with all that trim on his hat and the gold stars and gold stripes running up his sleeves.

The next two people out were army generals. This did not go over very well with the team or the commander. She stopped when she saw them and turned around, placing me so that she was between the helicopter and me. I looked back over my shoulder as she took me back to my home. She was fuming mad, and with her, that meant she became deathly quiet. While we were walking, she said in her wrist communicator, "Full alert. Watch, I want to know every movement, both inside and outside this compound. Team, if you see anything out of the ordinary, I want to know about it now. I want those two generals"—she spat out the word—"under the barrel of a gun at all times. Take the civilians and the nonessential personnel inside. Scramble!"

I don't think the generals liked it very much, being forced onto their knees, hands behind their heads, and with a cocked 9 mm pistol pressed against the backs of their necks. The admiral shouted orders that the team ignored. The president was not happy about guns being suddenly pointed in her direction either. Melanie dropped to her knees, closed her eyes, and started crying. Katie yelled to me, mentally, *"Get my niece out of there!"* I teleported Melanie to my home porch so she was away from the guns. I said through the window, "Don't worry, Melanie. They won't hurt you." She looked surprised, and so did everyone else.

The commander said, "How did she do that?" The commander was so upset that Melanie could just disappear and reappear wherever she wanted that she pulled her gun. She had it cocked and was about to pull the trigger, but I placed my hand on her arm and said, "I did it, Susan. She was so scared, and I know that she's not here to harm me. She's Katie's niece, and Katie yelled to get her away from there, so I did."

Melanie knelt on the porch, trembling, so I looked at Colleen and said, "She needs comforting."

Colleen immediately went outside and kneeled next to Melanie, while talking slowly and quietly, letting her know that no one wanted to harm her. "You're safe here."

The commander let the rest of the team in on what had happened, and then she turned to me to chew me out. "Freddy, please try to let us know when you're going to pull something like that. You scared me half to death, and I almost shot the child out of a need to protect you."

I looked up at her, threw my arms around her waist, and started crying. I don't know why I felt so relieved, but I did. She reached down and hugged me.

"I love you, Susan."

"I love you too, sweetheart. You need to remember that our training is very much reactive, and you may not have time to stop what you set into motion next time. Please think before you act. Okay?"

"I'll try. I'll try real hard."

"Good. Now let's take care of what's going on. Maggie, get to the house, and cover Freddy. Home, Shop, protect Freddy as per Order Five." The commander headed back toward the helicopter.

"*Affirmative,*" Shop responded.

"*Affirmative,*" Home echoed.

I looked at the watch. "What's Order Five?"

Marian said, "Order Five is for Home, Shop, and all resources to be stationed at full alert. All focused on protecting you. If Home or Shop detects anyone or anything that may harm you, they're dead. If anyone enters this command base, or if someone on the base enters the house or the workshop without the direct permission of an authorized person, or if someone tries to tamper with any part of the base, shop, or house, the computers will notify us and destroy them without question."

"The commander set that up?"

Marian laughed. "No, she ordered Maggie to do it. The commander is not very good with computers. She can run them, but programming and fixing them is not her forte."

"You said *all* resources?"

"Yes."

"Home … Shop … do not harm anyone under any orders

given except mine at this time. Order Five is for watching and reporting only."

"*Understood. Shop powering down Stingers and destroyer.*"

"*Home powering down lasers. Weapon systems powering down. Satellite weapons powering down.*"

Marian's eyes went wide, and her mouth hung open as she looked at me with astonishment. I put my finger to my lips and said, "Don't tell."

Colleen brought Melanie into the house. "Freddy, this is Melanie Orgonna."

Melanie looked at me and smiled a little. I put out my hand, and she took it. "Thank you for getting me away. Please don't harm my boss."

I said, "It's not up to me. Please tell Katie that you're all right before she blows a gasket and takes it out on that general she has under her gun."

She looked blank for a second, and I could feel Katie relax just a little and the pain recede from the general, as the gun was backed off enough to allow the blood to flow to the back of his head again.

The commander was just about at the helicopter, and she was still fuming. When she came up among the generals, she saluted the admiral and turned to the president. "I have only one question, Madam President. Please give me a reason why I should not shoot these two right here and now. You received my orders to them. Any person affiliated with the army who sets foot within ten miles of Freddy is dead, and so is the general in charge of them. I thought that order was simple enough."

I was shocked. I looked at Colleen and asked, "Did she really send a death threat to the army?"

"No, it was more like a promise. I'd like to know what's going on, Freddy. Please repeat what's being said."

"The president is about to answer."

"Commander James, please believe me when I say that I am the one who invited them here. I need this straightened out before it comes to bloodshed. It was very upsetting to receive their spy back with changes to his anatomy." I giggled, but she continued. "These two are the top generals in the army, and I don't need a war between the army and the navy. The losses on both sides would be extreme and would destroy this country."

I pathed to Katie, "*Quick—tell the commander that I just said it would be a quick and very one-sided battle.*"

"Commander? Freddy wants you to know that it would be a very quick and one-sided battle."

The commander turned back to the president. "You want Freddy to invent a way to take us to the stars. Let me tell you that he hates violence, but Katie tells me that he thinks the army would lose very quickly, and the navy would have few, if any, casualties. I'm not looking for a war, Madam President. I'm trying to do my job."

"I understand, Commander."

"I'm not sure you do, Madam President. Several months ago, I learned that Freddy believes the world is in big trouble. He's building something that will protect us all from what he thinks is total destruction. He works himself nearly to death. He doesn't need these army-related distractions, and I'm going to make damn sure that he doesn't have them anymore. I owe it to you, the country, and the world."

"He knows about the meteor, then?"

"Yes, he does. I only have a feeling; hopefully, you have more to tell us."

"It's big, Commander. The size of California, with ten times the mass. It's estimated that it will just miss Earth, but it's big enough to change our rotation and push us out of orbit. All life will stop. We didn't know until we started using his scanners. They clearly show the beast."

Colleen looked at me, startled. "Is this true, Freddy? Are we about to be hit by a huge meteor?"

"Oh, not for another two years. Wait until you get to scenario number sixty. The big problem is, I only have six more months to stop it, or even I won't have the ability without causing other problems."

"Then you're attempting to do something?"

I looked at her and said quietly, "Why do you think I've been working so hard? Do you really think I enjoy working three or four days without food or rest, over and over again, for months?" I looked back outside. "Quiet now, please."

The president said, "We have nothing that can stop it. We could fire all our missiles, but even if we could hit it, which is not likely, we wouldn't move it one inch. Not at the speed it's coming. Commander, it's moving faster than the speed of light. Very few people know about it, and we need to keep it that way. We've looked at everything and everyone. Freddy is our only hope, and the world can't afford for him to be sick in bed due to the stupid, foolish, childish maneuvers of the army. I came here to reassure Freddy that I will—and that these two generals will—make sure that he gets anything and everything he needs. Any help ..." She had tears in her eyes. "These two have come because they are willing to give their lives, right now, if that will get Freddy back to work. If it will make Freddy believe us, then I'll take that gun and shoot them and me right now. We have loved ones too, and we're scared. The vice president is ready to take over if we don't return, and his orders are to help you in every way possible. Please, Commander. Let me talk to Freddy. Let me beg him to help us."

"What do you think, Freddy? I know you're listening."

I pathed to her, *"She's telling the truth, and the generals are with her on this. Ask her if I can look deeper."*

"Freddy wants to know if he can have permission to look deeper into your mind, Madam President."

"Yes, anything."

I paused, thinking.

Melanie asked, *"Aren't you going to look?"*

"Katie, please tell her that I don't believe in raping minds. If she's that willing for me to look, then I don't need to. And tell her for me: welcome to our home."

The commander called, "Stand down, and resume normal duties for visitors. Madam President, Freddy says that he doesn't need to look into your mind. He can see you'd let him, and that's enough. He also says welcome to our home." She moved back to the generals, and as she allowed them to stand up, she said, "I'm sorry, sirs, but you understand."

"We understand, and thank you. Please tell Freddy that we're very sorry for frightening him, and thank him for not ordering our executions."

"He would never do that, General; that's my job," she said with steely eyes. "You're alive because Freddy says that the president is telling the truth and has welcomed her. That means it would be slightly rude to shoot the people she brought with her. On the other hand, please understand that I don't trust you, and you will be watched at all times." She turned to the admiral and said in a pleasant voice, "Nice to have you aboard, sir. Everyone, please come up to the house."

✦

Yellows said, "She is a Black. No wonder it was so difficult to grab her."

Everything went black, almost. I sensed the little Yellows' astonishment, and then it all went black completely.

Gray said, "Difficult! She killed eighteen of our best in the attempt. We should have never let this 'Commander Susan' go. A Black is the only creature that can kill our royalty. She has that ability and would have used it with her royalty, or 'president,' and they would allow it. She can only be a natural Black." Gray looked at me differently. "He has been surrounded by Blacks for years. The Grays renounce calling him weak."

Green said, "Our Reds are often surrounded by Grays but never Blacks. That would drive them to suicide. Yet he considers them pen mates."

The little Yellows said, "We don't think we understand their relationships. Theirs seem to be far deeper than ours. Please, let us continue."

✦ ✦ ✦

CHAPTER 14

APOLOGIES

They headed toward the house but had to pass the two shuttles to do so. The president was impressed, and so were the generals. One said, "It's too bad that the navy gets all the ships."

The admiral asked, "Do they actually fly in space?"

The commander replied, "You need to ask Freddy that question. Just for your information, not everything Freddy has invented is for the navy. But it will take some talking to get him to trust you enough to let them loose."

I pathed, *"Now, how did she know that! Katie?"*

"Yes, Freddy?"

"Are you peeking into my mind?"

"Stop thinking out loud when you're inventing. You know I can't block yet."

"Remind me to teach you."

"Thank you for saving my niece."

"You're welcome, but next time, let's warn the commander first." I showed her why.

She laughed one of those "thank God it didn't happen" kind of little laughs.

Everything must have been too much, as my legs gave out. Colleen grabbed me before I hit the floor.

"What's wrong, Freddy?" Melanie asked, worried.

Colleen said quietly, "He needs to sit down. His little legs are very weak after all that work, then worry, then depression, which caused him to sleep for the last four days without food or water, and now all this excitement. It's a wonder he's been able to stay standing this long."

"Was I really asleep for four days?"

"Yes, Freddy, and we were very worried. I'm going to leave you here with Maggie. You need some water, so I'll be right back. Don't you dare argue with me or tell me that you're not thirsty."

"But I'm ..." I saw a look of stubbornness cross her face and knew that I'd lose this time, so I said, "Thanks."

She smiled and left for the kitchen, saying, "That's better."

She came back out in less than a minute. "Dinner is almost ready, so Cooky won't let me ruin your appetite, but she gave me this for you instead." It was cherry Kool-Aid, which is my favorite. "She says the sugar will do you good." She handed a second glass to Melanie.

"Thanks, ma'am," Melanie said.

"You're welcome, young lady. So you're Katie's niece? What are you doing here?"

"I can answer that." The president had just come inside with the admiral, the commander, the two generals, and half the SEAL team. "Hello, Freddy. I want to apologize face-to-face for my failure to put a stop to the army's interference. I'm very sorry."

I tried to stand up, but Colleen put a hand on my shoulder and said, "He's weak, Madam President. If he stands up right now, there's a good chance he'd fall right back down."

I put my hand out and said to the president, "Still friends?"

She happily took my hand. "Still friends and hopefully always will be. As you know by now, this is Melanie Orgonna, and she's a telepath. Freddy, when you showed us your ability to read minds, the government started looking really close at how they could protect me."

"I would never harm you."

"Not protection from you, Freddy. With you, we were very lucky. We had a kind, morally stable American who wants nothing more than to invent and build. This is a quote from the FBI report I received on you: 'A kind kid who would never harm anyone intentionally.' Think, though—what if it was a spy? What if the telepath was from a hostile country, or what if he or she had no morals regarding scanning my mind? This country would be in deep trouble. The FBI had no solution until you gave us one."

"Me?"

"That's right. When you came to see me the last time, you said that I should have my own telepath to help me know when someone was lying to me."

"I remember that very clearly. It was just after the meeting with those congressmen. They lied a lot."

"Yes, they did, but because you were there, they had to tell the truth—and every bit of it. That saved us a lot of trouble and made honest men of them all—for at least a little while. The FBI decided to find someone with this capability, so they did a nationwide search. Freddy, you wouldn't believe how many people can receive or transmit using telepathy."

"Being a telepath, yes, I would."

"That's true, but you know that most are not strong enough to actually do anything with it?"

I said, "Most people burn themselves out and can never

use it again. When emotions run high, like when telepaths become hurt or come close to dying, those people transmit with everything they have on a wide range. They don't do it on purpose. They don't even know they can. It just happens. Others who are especially close to them receive just enough to understand something has happened. I'm sure all of us have heard of people who have known that someone close to them was in trouble, even if that person was across town. Many people have this experience but usually only once with an individual, as the individual burns himself or herself out on that initial burst of sending. That's why I need to stay away from big cities as much as possible. My shields tend to come down a little when I sleep and relax. Each time they burn themselves out, I hear it and wake up. It drives me nuts."

She smiled. "That's exactly how we found most of our candidates to be. We looked for people who complained that they were hearing things. We put some of them together and found out that a few could talk with each other telepathically. Some could only receive, and some could only transmit. On that initial search we found only three who could do both. We were too late for all three of them, as they were already insane.

"The FBI started looking into children then. Over the last six months, we've found hundreds of children who have potential. Melanie, here, is the best and most stable. Freddy, she has already pointed out several people who are telepaths who were spying on us. We've been using her to clean up this issue. I take her with me to most meetings. She is still underage, and there is a protection group that is monitoring us very closely to ensure we don't take advantage of her or any of the children. They stay with their parents whenever possible, and now that we know what to do, we're doing things to ensure they don't go insane also. These kids are a national resource, and we need them desperately, now that we know that other countries are doing the same thing and using them as spies."

Katie came in and put an arm around her niece. They were talking mentally, bringing each other up-to-date. The president continued. "One of the things that Melanie brought up was just what you said. The city is no place for a child telepath to live. We've moved many of them and their families out to the country, at the government's expense." She looked at the generals. "However, I'm being rude by continuing this conversation. We can talk about this later. Right now, I'd like you to meet Chief of Operations General Alan Slaven. He is the top rank in the army."

I looked at him coldly with eyes narrowed.

"Dr. Anderson," he said. "I am truly sorry that in the past I have not been able to maintain cooperation in my ranks. Please be assured that steps have been taken to ensure that this will not happen again."

"I like that, sir, and I like your use of the word 'I' versus 'they,' which means that you're taking responsibility for what has happened. That makes me feel like the problem may be over. I hope it is and will treat it as such, but please understand that you're going to have to earn my trust."

"I understand, and I think I would feel the same way, Dr. Anderson. Let me introduce you to my second in command, General Raff Tankman. He and his family have been in the army for seven generations."

I looked at him. "You poor man. You have my sympathy."

Susan smiled inside but said, "Freddy, don't be discourteous."

I bowed my head and said, "I'm sorry, General. It was just such a good setup line, and I couldn't help myself."

The general smiled at the commander. "Well, sometimes

I feel the same way. It's difficult to live up to the expectations of others when your family history is full of heroes."

The president said, "This is Fleet Admiral Martin Pinn."

I put out my hand. "Nice to meet you, sir. Do you think I could talk you into helping the commander find some really great pilots? I need some with very quick reflexes who can work in three-dimensional situations with no gravity. We're going to need a large complement of people to run my destroyer and all the toys that go with it."

"Nice to finally meet you too, Dr. Anderson. Yes, I'll help in any way I can."

"Great! I'll show you what I mean." I tried to get up, but my legs were still wobbly.

Colleen guided me back down onto the chair. "It can wait until you're better. Calm down, Freddy. Stop getting excited. The admiral can wait until tomorrow to see your toys. You can discuss them with him tonight after dinner, if you want, but you won't be going outside to do anything until I think you can stand up on your own."

"Yes, ma'am."

I saw the commander flash Colleen a sign. Colleen helped me stand and said, "It will be time for dinner soon, so let's go wash up. You didn't get behind your ears very well, and I need you to concentrate on slowly finishing that Kool-Aid."

I put my arm around her waist and said, "I'll be right back. It was very nice meeting all of you."

Once I was upstairs, the conversation changed. The commander started off. "Admiral, Freddy's very easy to get along with and loves to show people his 'toys.' The problem is that he doesn't know when to stop. I'm sorry."

"No need to apologize. That child is very precocious and unreserved, isn't he? You seem to have a good handle on him. How do you do it?"

"You left out extremely tenacious and highly dangerous

to himself. We've saved his life three times over the last six months. He gets to working on something and walks off cliffs or into helicopter blades. Watching him is a twenty-four-hours-a-day, 365-days-a-year job. He has no sense of time and will come out of the shop at midnight, wondering why it's dark. As to your question, it's easy." She looked at the generals and said, "We don't do anything to ruin his trust in us. He loves and trusts everyone naturally, until they harm him or try to do something bad to him. Violate his trust, and that's it. He never forgets, but he forgives quickly, so you have a chance, generals. Don't blow it."

Katie said, "He's coming back down."

✦

Blue said, "Interesting bit of fact. We can use that."

Everything went black. I thought, *Good! About time they started talking. Now for some fun.*

Yellows said, "What did you gain in that?"

Blue answered, "We can gain the trust and friendship of their top scientist if we simply do as this 'commander' stated. 'Don't do anything to ruin his trust.' This is an easy thing to do."

Green said, "He would not have this problem if his entire race were telepathic. It took hundreds of years before we learned to lie while in telepathic bond."

The bigger Yellows snapped Green hard with a tentacle. "And did he just hear you announce that we have the ability to lie?"

Green exclaimed, while rubbing his head, "Oh no, I did not think." Yet his emotions screamed, *I will not allow them to deceive a Red!*

Yellows looked at Green skeptically and ordered, "Continue."

CHAPTER 15

✦ ✦ ✦

DINNER

The commander quickly finished her statement. "Remember at all times that this 'child' is the smartest person on the planet. He is highly empathic, and if you lie, or tell half-truths, or try to deceive him in any way, he will know it before you finish the sentence." She turned to the admiral. "He trusts you enough to show you his 'toys,' and that's amazing. Believe me when I say this: it has nothing to do with his needing us because I can assure you that he doesn't. At least, not for running his toys."

"Why does he let you stay here and guard him, then?" asked the general.

"At first, he allowed us to stay so that he could test us and gain more time in his shop. He's very worried about that meteor. Now, he keeps us here because he loves us." She smiled. "And that comes with trust. We happen to love him too, and we'd follow him anywhere." Standing straighter and in a louder voice, she said proudly, "We're going to the stars with him."

"Any idea how many people he needs?"

"No, but I know we're not enough. I don't know what

kinds of expertise he needs either. You'll have to talk to him about that."

The admiral asked, "What does this destroyer look like? How big is it?"

"I don't know, sir. He lets me into the front section of the shop but not deep into his work area. He says that it's dangerous. I don't even know how big his work area is. The scanners can't penetrate it, for some reason. We do know this: there is a section under the mountain that is five miles long and three miles wide that we can't see, and when I'm in the front of the shop, I can hear a tremendous amount of work going on through what must be hundreds of feet of solid rock."

The conversation stopped. Everyone looked up, as Colleen was bringing me down the stairs. Just about that time, Cooky came out and said, "Dinnertime."

We filed into the dining room. All of the leaves were in the table so there was plenty of room, but most of the SEAL team stayed around the edges, watching. The commander had several of the team sit down and join us. I was sandwiched between Maggie and Betsy, and it was made very clear why they sat next to me. The commander was taking no chances. All the aerospace personnel and the FAA inspector were introduced. The president sat at one end of the table, and the commander sat at the other.

Mr. Fly, the inspector, cut right through the small talk. "What was all that about earlier? I nearly messed my pants."

The commander answered, "We were not expecting the army or the navy to be included on this trip. We don't like surprises."

The president said, "That was my fault. I was supposed to come alone but decided to bring these gentlemen and my young friend along as a pleasant surprise. I won't do that again."

Everyone laughed when Mr. Fly said, "I certainly hope not, Madam President. These ladies frisked me and interrogated me pretty heavily when I came here, but at least I didn't almost get my backside shot off."

Dinner looked good, and my appetite was coming back, so I ate quite a bit. When I realized that almost everyone was watching me, I whispered to Maggie, "Did I do something wrong?"

"No, dear. We're just glad your appetite's back."

I blushed and slowed down after that and joined the conversation. Petty Officer Henry Peters was sitting across from me. "Henry, what do you think of my home so far?"

He smiled. "Scary"—and then, after a second of thought— "and exciting." Henry wasn't much for talk. I had the feeling that he considered anything except organizational paperwork a total waste of time.

I looked over at PN3 Dorothy Pendelson and asked her the same thing.

She answered enthusiastically, "Freddy, I've never had so much excitement. I am totally enjoying myself. I've seen espionage, worked with people who have been to the moon, studied sciences and math that I had no idea were possible, met the president of the United States, and almost saw her get shot—legally, of course. Generally, I'd say I've had the time of my life, but the worst part is that I can't tell anyone! Darn."

Everyone laughed except the president. She was very serious. I looked at her and asked, "Madam President, you want me to help with a mutual problem we seem to have—a big rock that we can't duck."

She said yes on a whisper of air, as if saying it out loud would cause the meteor to hit sooner.

"I've worked all my life on this project. I've known about that rock for years, but no one would believe me."

"We believe you now," she said.

"Thank you. The bad thing is, I only have six months to stop it. After that, I will not be able to stop it. The good thing is, I should be able to handle that if I'm allowed to do things in my own way."

"We're doomed," said the admiral. "Nothing exists that could reach that meteor within eighteen months, and that's if we launch now."

I looked at the admiral and said, "Nothing that you have, but the longer we wait, the closer the meteor gets. Even I can't stop the problems its gravity will create after a certain point. The issue now is to get to it within the next six months."

He looked at me and said, "With all due respect, I don't see how those two shuttles can do enough harm to stop that thing."

I thought for a minute. "That's an idea, I suppose. I could send them up to destroy it. They have the ability, but that would be a waste of two perfectly good shuttles and their crews."

He leaned in, looking upset, and said, "You're joking."

Susan said, "Admiral, he never jokes about his work— never. If Freddy says that the two shuttles out there can destroy that meteor, then believe me, they can."

The president asked, "If the shuttles can do the job, please let's use them—now."

"I will keep them as an emergency backup if needed, but it's a suicide mission for two brave crews. I would do that to save the world, of course, but I don't see the need. Even if I could not get my project finished in time, those two shuttles have the ability to reach that rock in a matter of a few hours."

General Tankman asked, "Even if they can reach it, how can two little ships destroy that thing when five hundred nuclear multitipped missiles would hardly scratch it? That's enough to destroy this planet several times over."

I looked at him and replied, "Sir, I can destroy this planet completely using only one of those ships and the cargo I can place on it for delivery. The only reason I would need two ships for this job is that one has to slow it down enough for the second one to destroy it."

His eyes went wide and his mouth hung open in astonishment. "You can do that?"

"Why do you think I don't want people spying on me? As soon as that thing is destroyed, so will be the knowledge of how I can do this. The ships will remain for my projects, but the missiles I have built will be gone—and all the knowledge with it. If this happens again, then I can always reinvent them but not unless something extremely drastic like this happens."

"Why don't you just give us the equipment and let us do the job?" asked the admiral.

"Because you have all kinds of security problems—and you don't have a clue about many of your problems. If I let you in on my missile-building knowledge, then in a year, every major power on this planet will have the ability to win in a first strike. Do you want that?"

He sat back and thought for a second. "No, I don't. And you're right. It would leak, and then we'd all be speaking another language."

"No, Admiral, we wouldn't exist. Someone else would have to move in after they replanted and rebuilt, but it would not harm the rest of the planet, so what do they have to lose? A terrorist group could sit back and hit every major power and be the only ones left on the planet. I think they'd like that. We, on the other hand, are not the kind of people to use it first. However, others would love to get rid of us 'immoral Westerners.' No. I will keep the knowledge to myself. Not even the commander has any idea, and I trust her and this team with my life. No telepath on the planet has the ability to take it from me." I pointed to my head. "It's locked up so well that it takes hours for me to access it from my own mind. They could rape my mind until I was just a vegetable and still not get a clue. My shop is shielded, so they can't get it that way either."

"And if you die before the job is completed?" asked the president.

I looked at her and shrugged my shoulders.

"Oh God," said Colleen. "I think our job just became considerably more important. It's not just protecting the kid we all love so much. Now it's protecting everyone we love. It's saving the whole planet."

I looked at her and said, "It's not just a job; it's an adventure, isn't it?"

Betsy quickly became upset. "No! This is not funny, Freddy. This isn't a comic book. This is our lives we're talking about, and I don't think I'll sleep again until that thing is blown to bits."

I looked at her. "I'm going to have to start reading comic books. They sound interesting."

The president asked, "Freddy, what are you going to do?"

"If I can get the correct help, I fully plan to rip it apart and either disintegrate it entirely or push the rest toward the sun. Then I'll return here and continue with my other projects."

"How are you going to do that?"

"With the destroyer I've almost finished building, a select crew, and my teammates. The destroyer is very capable of stopping that tiny little rock. After it's destroyed, I will stay around long enough to get what I need from the rock and then send the large debris, if any, on another path into the sun or someplace where it won't cause issues. There may be a mess to clean up so no chunks hit the earth."

The admiral asked, "When can we see this destroyer? What is it?"

"It's a medium-sized ship about the size of two of your aircraft carriers. It's built specifically as an escort for other ships that are taking long voyages. I hadn't planned on building any protection ships until I had some working ships first, but the requirements have changed. You have to be flexible when working on a long-term project."

"You have a ship that big inside that mountain?"

"Actually, I'm working on a much bigger ship right next to it. It's my newest toy. A ship big enough to take buildings to the moon and Mars. You can't build everything out in space or in a hostile environment, you know—far too expensive. I figure that we can build houses, offices, and factories here on platforms. Then we just pick them up and take them wherever we want them."

The admiral asked, "How many people do you need to run this 'destroyer'?"

"I don't know. I haven't thought about it much. I was hoping to finish all the essential stuff, and then bring it out and have people tell me what I missed in the way of comforts and necessities, and then we could find out how many people we need."

"You were asking about pilots?"

"Yes." I turned a little red. "I was trying to invent robots to run most of the stuff, but I failed."

"Freddy! I don't believe it!" exclaimed Marian. "You failed at something?"

Colleen gave her a dirty look and said to me, "We're all human, sweetheart."

I smiled up at Colleen and looked at Marian. "The only reason I failed is because I cannot get the materials I need to build them. Platinum is expensive, and to make them would take me four months. That is far too much time for the current project. Also, I don't like the idea of building artificial intelligence, and that's what it would take."

The admiral cleared his throat. I looked over at him and said, "I'm sorry, Admiral, back to your question. The answer isn't simple, but I do know that we need twenty pilots to fly the Stingers, six three-person teams with pilots for the six Sting Rays, four eight-person teams for the four shuttles, and about four ten-person teams to run the bridge of the destroyer. Then there's the engineering section, the medical section, the weapons section, the science areas, the cargo bay and hangar bay crews, a maintenance crew, and communications and personnel support people. I think we could run it effectively with a minimal crew of about three hundred. It needs to be run twenty-four/seven, so that includes three separate crews, with eight hours on and sixteen off. I would really suggest eight to nine hundred people. The reason I say I can't estimate how many are required is because I'm not an expert on manpower, but the commander is." I looked over at her and smiled. "I trust her to figure it out or to find someone who can."

"Thank you, Freddy," said Susan.

"I know my limitations, Admiral. I don't run this household; the commander does, because she's much better at it than I am. I can't run everything and get anything done on my projects, so she handles everything except the inventing and building, which includes determining the required manpower, getting them here, and training them. I wouldn't even be going on this trip if I had the time to train people in everything and could trust them as much as I trust the commander. But I can't, so I have to go. This is going to take more time away from my other projects, but that can't be helped. I can't trust others at this time, so I'm taking my bodyguards with me, and I will train them to run things, if it becomes necessary. They can teach others."

"Freddy, can you explain about the ships you mentioned, please?" asked the president.

I looked at the generals and then back to the president. "No, not right now. I'm sorry."

The two generals looked at each other and then at the admiral. "Freddy, if I vouch for them, would you have a little more trust?" asked the admiral,

Sadly, I answered, "No. Please don't get me wrong, sir. I would love to trust them, but I don't. If I was maybe a little more grown up and had more life experience, I could find it easier to forgive and trust, but I'm still a kid, and I don't have the wisdom that comes with time. The commander helps a lot with my deficiency in this area and tries to keep me from doing things that would upset the president." I looked at the president and smiled. "I hope it is working."

She said, "Don't worry, Freddy. You're doing great."

"I am achieving edification from the team, Madam President. Nevertheless, my present project consumes an ardent apportionment of operational opportunity that has—"

"Freddy!"

Startled, I looked at Colleen.

"You're doing it again. Stop it!"

I blushed, "I'm sorry, Madam President. What I meant to say is that I'm learning a lot from the girls, but my time is being used up, working on this emergency instead of having the benefit of their teaching on a continuous basis. It's sporadic at best. The commander does a great job, but the circumstances that this emergency is creating have caused both of us to deviate off a most favorable solution to my upbringing."

The president smiled. "Every once in a while, you let slip with just how intelligent you are." When I blushed, she said, "That's not a bad thing, Freddy. Not as long as someone is here to remind you that we may not understand." She nodded her thanks to Colleen, who nodded back.

I sat in deep thought for a minute, and then I looked at the commander and with a big smile said, "Susan, I'd like to make the admiral a trade."

"What would that be, Freddy?"

"This is all dependent on what you think of the idea—if you feel we should talk first, or if we should wait until the generals are gone or whatever."

"Depends on what you want to do."

"I would like to take you, the president, and Melanie, plus as many of the team as you feel is necessary, with me into the shop. I'll let you see firsthand what I've been working on, and that way you may have a better understanding of the needs we face."

"In return for what?"

"Two things. First, I want the admiral to help the team in any way you deem necessary, including personnel, equipment, supplies, building materials, Earth communications, logistics for transport, screening, etc. I seem to be running out of easily available funds. I'm still very rich, but I get the payments for my patents on a monthly or yearly basis, and I quickly use up most of that income each month and then have to wait to buy the supplies I need. I don't want to be indebted to anyone, so this is for free, and the ships are still mine." I paused for a minute and then burst out laughing.

Everyone was smiling or laughing with me, including the commander. "What's so funny?" she asked.

"Commander, I just realized what I was saying. As if I would want them back, cluttering up this base. And what about the fact that I need the president to continue supporting my projects? So let's amend my request. I want insurance that the ships I design will be used to help build a city on the moon, another one on Mars, and eventually will allow us travel to the stars. As long as I am not held back from achieving those goals, then you can use them for anything else you want. Second, I want to learn to trust the generals and the army, which means I need to work with them. To do so, I need someone I can trust to screen their people before they are sent here, where you then can screen them again, Commander. That way, maybe you won't have them shot on sight. Right now, we don't much like the army. Sorry, generals. We really need to change that. If we can't work together, then this job is going to be a lot harder, and my projects will take a lot longer." I looked over at the generals and said, "Please don't get me wrong. I'm going to the moon and Mars, and I'm going to land on another planet and breathe air that's not from Earth. I can do it alone or with help, but I will do it. Susan, Colleen, and the rest of this team have shown me how important it is to have companions I can trust. I would very much prefer going with my friends. Susan, what do you think?"

"I don't know, Freddy. Let me think about it." She spoke with such a straight face, yet I could feel the mirth radiating from her. The president's eyes were popping out with disbelief that Susan would not grab at the chance, and the admiral was about to come out of his chair and read her the riot act. The two team members who were suddenly standing directly behind him put a stop to that idea.

Susan said, "I would love to allow Freddy this opportunity to give us all a tour, but I cannot."

Everyone started talking at once—the admiral, the generals, everyone except the president, but only because Melanie had a hand on her arm, suggesting that she wait. When things calmed down, Susan continued. "The reason for this is we must wait until Freddy and I have put away any and all things that may give anyone a clue about how he is building those bombs. I will not compromise that technology. When we have done that, then I will be happy to allow you in. I think we should include the generals, though. If we show a little good faith, then possibly they can return the favor."

Both acknowledged agreement.

The admiral calmed down and asked, "Freddy, how long will it take to clear things up so that we can see the ships?"

"Just a second, Admiral. Shop?"

"*Yes, Freddy. I take it you wish for me to remove from sight all items pertaining to the development and building of missiles and mass-destruction weapons. Is this correct?*"

"Yes, and I would like to remove all hazards that could cause harm to people who have no understanding of the physical nature and properties of robots. Please have two BRGs standing by to escort the generals and GRPs for the rest. I will be there right after dinner with the commander to inspect and make adjustments."

"*Understood. Everything will be ready.*"

"Thank you."

The admiral was still looking around for the voice.

The commander said, "Sir, the voice won't come back unless someone with the proper authority calls her. 'Thank you' signals that the conversation is over."

"Interesting. Will there be a computer with that style of input/output on the ships?"

"No, sir," I responded. "I'd never populate my new ships with old technology."

Everyone's eyebrows rose.

General Tankman asked, "Exactly what are BRGs and GRPs?"

"Oh sorry, General. BRG is short for Blue Robot Guard, and GRP is short for Green Robot Protector."

"What's the difference between the two?"

"GRP is a nice little energy that follows you around, and helps explain things, and generally keeps you from harming yourself by giving passive warnings."

"And the BRG?"

"The Blue Robot Guard is an active system. I haven't gotten all the bugs out of it yet, but it's supposed to watch you, and if it sees you doing something that you shouldn't, it disintegrates you and tells me later, when I'm not busy. Susan, we should be able to check the shop, and then sometime tomorrow morning we can give the tour."

The generals' eyes were the size of plates. I ignored them. I looked over at the president. "Madam President, can you stay for a tour tomorrow?"

"I would be honored."

"One other thing—sometime soon the knowledge of that rock is going to be leaked. Then what? I don't want visitors who are a hindrance to my progress. No reporters without the commander giving the clearance for who, where, and when."

"Freddy, you're in my territory again," Susan reminded me. "Don't worry about it. I'll handle everything."

I looked at Susan. "I just want to make it clear not to tell anyone that the solution is coming from here. I'd like to keep that a secret until we launch. It would be a shame if some fanatic group decided to try to stop us for some off-the-wall reason. The last thing I want is to have to attend funerals just before lifting off. Next question. Susan, the girls who are training with the shuttle mockup—where are they in terms of scenarios?"

Marian answered, "We're at number forty-nine. Been there for two days now."

"Really? What's the problem?"

"We've had some dogfights in other scenarios, but we

were not expecting to have to do battle with a huge ship. Isn't this just a little ridiculous? The girls are starting to think you don't want them to pass."

"Really? Shop?"

"*Yes, Freddy?*"

"When was the last scan of the solar system completed?"

"*Two hours and sixteen minutes ago.*"

"Please give me an update on traffic, other than known satellites."

"*There are eight small-class ships taxiing in and out of the system. Five have visited the ship based deep in the Pacific Ocean. One medium-sized ship, thought to be a supply ship, has left high orbit. No other traffic noticed. I have compiled the known information of activities and believe that I now understand what is happening with the increased traffic. The base ship is preparing to leave.*"

"Thank you. So our benefactors are leaving. I would bet they know exactly what's coming. What I don't know is if they made it happen or if they simply can't stop it. Either way, they're leaving before things get bad. I do not want to believe that they're responsible for this problem. I know for a fact that they have saved our planet several times. At least, all signs point to them. However, I don't want to take the chance. When we let the world know about my project, they'll know too. Therefore, we hold off as long as possible. When we launch, they will know, and they will have the ability to try to stop us, but I'm not launching until we can protect ourselves. That'll be in about four months. At that time, I will be able to protect this base from anything, and then we're going for a test ride. I want to see if my systems work as they should."

Everyone was staring at me except the president and the admiral; they were looking guilty.

"I can feel your emotions. You both knew."

"We do have a craft that was disabled," said the admiral.

"The craft you have at Area 51 is not theirs, Admiral. You have other information, and if you found the rock, then you must have picked up on the traffic."

"That's correct," said the president. "We simply had no idea what to do about it. That was one of the things we needed to talk to you about, but when we first reached this base, we had no idea that you even knew."

"Let alone that you were already working on the solution," added the admiral.

"You know we're going to have to address this issue, as it's not long now before we have first contact. Another thing— my ships are faster than theirs, they don't have shields, and my lasers are faster, as mine require no recharge." I turned to Marian and asked, "Are you using the shields?"

"Actually, no. We weren't sure if we could fire with them up."

"Did you see the button that toggles between 'one direction' and 'two direction' on the shield console?"

"Yes."

"It's in the two-direction position, isn't it?"

"Yes."

"The two-direction position is normal and shields both directions, in and out."

"And the one-direction position keeps things out but not in," she said. "Darn. We could use your help with a few issues sometime soon. I'll bet there are a dozen other things that we don't understand."

"You'll have that help as soon as you get to scenario fifty-one. By then, you'll have the simplest basics out of the way, and we can work on the really tough things together." I added with a mysterious smile, "I hope that at least one of you is very good at three-dimensional strategies. It'd be no fun if we died over and over." I stood up and raised my glass. "To the salvation of our world, the trust of good friends, and the love of the human race. Shields up."

We clinked glasses and drank; mine was milk. We finished dinner with just small talk and some unessential questions. After dinner, the commander and I went to the shop.

✦

Yellows smiled. "So the pending disaster was a meteor."

Everything went blank—they think. Number-one rule of all life: if you can't change the circumstances, then adapt or perish.

Green said, "No meteor showed up on our scans of their system or surrounding system."

Blue said, "It quoted four of it months. How long would that be?"

Green thought for a second. "About eighteen of our days."

"That's strange," said Gray. "Our mother ship should have been near their system by then. We received no reports of any meteors that would affect them."

Yellows said, "Maybe the mother ship was not looking."

Green said, "If he has world-destroying missiles, why did he not use them on our fleet?"

Yellows said, "Another mystery. Please continue."

PREPPING SHOP FOR HER FIRST VISITORS

Almost everyone followed us out to the cliff. When we reached the proper spot, on a tight beam so that Katie and Melanie would not detect it, I triggered the proper sequence inside to open the shield wall. The commander and I walked through the wall, and the shield slammed into place.

"Shop?"

"*Yes, Freddy? Hello, Commander.*"

"Hello, Shop."

"Give me a video of the outside of this wall, please," I said.

On the wall appeared a video of the admiral and the two generals, trying to find the opening. The girls were laughing at them. Everyone else had seen this a hundred times. The president had Melanie off to one side. She said, "I don't know if you caught how he did that, but don't tell anyone. It's important to the security of the world that no one gets the information inside that shop until Freddy is ready to give it out."

"He is much stronger than I am and probably would have sensed it if I had tried. I did not try because you ordered me to not pry. I like his sense of morals on this subject, and I think I'm going to adopt them. No prying unless it's absolutely necessary, but I can't shut out the open mind."

I was happy that the young lady had the scruples of her aunt. I pathed to Katie and told her what I'd heard. She was happy too. I told the commander what I'd heard and let her know that it made me feel a little better.

"Shop, open up the back areas completely. We'll be doing a tour of the build complex. Attach a YRP to the commander, please."

"Freddy, I have to remind you that a Yellow Robot Protector only warns once and does not protect."

I looked at the commander and said, "I understand, Shop. I think the commander is quite capable, and I trust her to not get into trouble."

A yellow light about the size of my thumb showed up and hovered near the commander's right ear, just outside her peripheral vision. She turned her head, but the dot followed so quickly she couldn't see it.

"Where'd it go?"

"It's next to your right ear. Put your hand up, and you can get it to move forward."

She did, and the yellow dot was just within sight as it zoomed around her head to get out of the way and then resumed hovering near her right ear.

"If you don't like the position of the dot, simply ask it to move to another position."

"Dot, please move to my left side." The dot did as directed. "That's very neat, Freddy. What's it made of?"

"Energy. It's pure energy. The shop computer controls it."

"Dot, what are your orders?"

A tiny voice said in the commander's ear, "To warn if

you are about to do something that may harm you or if you may be about to harm the project."

"Could you hear that, Commander?" I asked.

"Yes. Very clearly."

"Good."

"Freddy, you said you didn't have all the bugs out of them yet?"

"I don't think we'll have a problem with the reds, greens, or yellows, but the blues tend to be a little overzealous regarding their responsibility, and I won't even turn on the blacks anymore. I lost five robots just because the blacks didn't like them looking at me when I walked by. At least the blues think first before they do anything."

✦

The Green choked for a second, trying to hold back controlled laughter.

Blue said in an annoyed tone, "I would continue, if I were you."

✦

We searched the entire front area and found some paperwork that the commander said I should put away, and then we headed toward the back. At the opening to my construction floor, the Commander paused. I could feel the astonishment and the pure delight radiating off her. The space was over five miles long and three miles wide. The walls, ceiling, and floor were of steel-hard granite, compressed and polished to a glassy sheen. The mirror-like reflections off the walls and ceiling made what was enormous look almost impossible. With all the activity, someone could stand at the opening and watch for days and never see everything.

Susan said in a whisper, "How?"

"It's easy. I built one robot to build and program robots that build and program other robots to build what I want built. I continually have to update the original and the others so that I can get new types of jobs completed, but I assure you that everything is completed exactly as I specify, using all the best materials and the best workmanship. These ships are not built by contractors who provided the cheapest bid."

"How did you even make this workshop?"

"You've seen me work with my equipment, making holes for the mini-homes and stuff. It's the same thing here, only there is a lot more planning involved and a lot more work."

"It's all so beautiful! I see so much going on, but I hear almost nothing."

"I designed the shop to have the worst acoustics possible. Get more than a few feet away from someone, and you have to yell. The dots will communicate between each person."

She turned to me with a mischievous grin. "Where's your dot, then?"

"Bit, show yourself." A clear dot changed colors through the spectrum and then returned to clear again.

"Is Bit always with you?"

"Only when I'm in the shop. As soon as I leave, she's not needed anymore. She can't leave the shop … not very far, anyway."

Susan looked back out over the mess. Robots were everywhere. Materials were stored everywhere. I had incorporated a lot of safety features into the shop so there was nothing stacked very high without bracing, and the walkways and exits were all marked and kept clear. I had over two thousand robots now, and they were quite a sight. Some moved slowly and some very fast, and many flew

JOHN RICKS

or hovered. They came in all sizes, shapes, and colors. Completed ships were set on racks stacked to one side, and the two main ships—the ones I was currently working on—were in the center. The destroyer was pointing at us, and directly to our left, dwarfing the destroyer, was a ship bigger by a factor of ten—my building-mover ship.

A thought crossed my mind, and I asked the commander, "Susan, since that ship is for moving things, do you think I could hire one of the moving-van companies to run it?"

She looked at me with unbelievable distaste and then saw how hard I was trying to keep from laughing. She gave my hair braid a little tug and laughed with me.

We took the platform to the bottom and walked into the shop. We searched the entire place. It took a long time to search the destroyer and each small ship because I had to stop to rest frequently. I thought we were taking this a little too far, but she insisted we check everything. The mover ship took almost no time at all, as it was still just a shell.

We finished around midnight and left the shop. During our tour, I told her about all of the issues that had come up and the things that I still had not figured out how to do. Most were things that any human could do, but getting a robot to understand and do it was a different thing entirely.

"Freddy, I know you don't want people in your shop, but if you'd let us help, most of your issues would go away."

"I know, Susan. After we remove that rock, I will let people into the shop to help. I have so much to do, and I can tell you right now I'm going to take a rest after this and then slow down. I have no problem farming out work and having people come in after that. Until then, I just can't take the chance."

"It's a lot of work, sweetheart. We should start calling you Noah."

I smiled. "When I build the Ark II, then they can call me

122

Noah. Until then, I'm just Freddy." With enthusiasm, I asked, "Did you know that I have already identified three planets that may be good for colonization?"

"I don't doubt it, but how did you do that?"

"I had to test out my drive system and shields, and I also had to test out my FTL communication system. I built several probes and sent them out at nearly 250 times the speed of light. Sounds fast, doesn't it? What it means is they crawl along at about one light-year every four minutes. I've been getting information back from them for five months now. I sent out one hundred of them, but I haven't had time to go over the data lately. I suppose I could give that information to someone to look at for me. Shop, give me a data chip on the information sent back from my Class One probes."

"*Working.*"

"Send it to the front office."

"*Will do, Freddy. It's a lot of information and will take three minutes to download onto a data chip.*"

"Three minutes! How much information is there?"

"*Approximately 157 billion gigabytes.*"

"That's a lot of information to sort through!" A smile crossed my face as I asked the commander, "That information is highly important, isn't it?"

"Yes, Freddy. I believe it would be. There could be vast amounts of information about the galaxies, stars, habitable planets, and other life forms." Her eyes narrowed. "Why?"

"The information is important and would make the people giving it out look very good, wouldn't it?"

"Yes, it would."

"If I gave this information to the army to investigate and study, wouldn't it take them a long time and possibly give them so much to do that they would stay out of our hair for a few months?"

She smiled. "Yes, it would." She paused, thinking.

"Freddy, let me handle the conversation. You just—very reluctantly—hand over the data cube when I tell you."

"Bad cop, good cop?"

"More like a parent telling a child to do something he doesn't want to do."

"I can play that real well." I took hold of her hand and added, "Mommy."

She smiled and said, "Don't overdo it. They're not that easy."

"Susan, this could actually be some of the greatest discoveries ever. The army will become very popular if this holds the information I think it does."

"I know—and that's why it will work. Let's go."

✦

Gray said, "He has information on systems in this area. We could use that."

The little Yellows tried to shut me down but failed. They tried again and failed.

Green said, "We have good maps of the area."

Gray said, "Not detailed like his. Ours are scanned from afar, and his are up close."

Yellows said, "Quiet! What is wrong, my friend?"

In a beginning panic, the little Yellows said, "We cannot shut it down. It has found a way around our shields."

The bigger Yellows reached in and did something unexpected. They tickled me. I lost concentration, and everything went black. Yellows said, "We learned that from one of their transmissions. We have used it on several of our own."

The little Yellows said, "They are ticklish as we are. How interesting that they could be so different, so ugly, and still be so much like us."

Yellows said, "Please continue, Green."

CHAPTER 17

✦ ✦ ✦

GIVING AWAY INFORMATION TO PROTECT WHAT YOU HAVE

We left the shop and headed back to the house. Two girls were waiting for us; one left with us, and one stayed at the invisible shop door. At the house we both said hello to Lieutenant Morgan, as she was waiting up for the commander. I picked up the data cube and left to clean up and go to bed. Just before I left the room, the commander said, "First thing in the morning is eight o'clock and no earlier, Freddy." I nodded my agreement. It's a good thing she said that, as I was thinking five o'clock. The hot shower felt great.

The alarm went off at seven thirty, and I slowly climbed out of bed and dressed. I was still very weak. Since I was going to the shop, I figured that a work jumper and my nonslip tennis shoes would be best. I was going to only tie my hair back, but I had the time, so I braided it like my mother use to braid hers. That took all of ten minutes. I brushed my teeth and went out. I slid down the banister and was caught at the bottom by the master chief. There I was, getting chewed out royally, when the president and Melanie came down.

I paid no attention to them, because when the master chief is ripping you a new one, you pay full attention to what she says, or your backside pays the price. I had learned that the hard way. She has a hand as hard as the knot in an old oak tree and an arm that never tires.

I took my reprimand, as I knew I had it coming. She had told me many times not to slide down that banister because I could get hurt, or worse yet, I could harm someone coming up the stairs. She was raised believing *"No horseplay in the house!* You want to fool around, you take it outside."

When she was finally winding down, she took me in her arms and helped me to stop crying. Hey, you'd cry too if you thought she was going to spank you right there in front of the president. She doesn't let you keep your pants on when she lays into you. I'm not sure where in the South she comes from, but when she gets mad she says things like "yeah, boys" and "ya don't know nuttin." I'd laugh, but I learned that that can be a very painful mistake. Besides, I become too scared to laugh.

After I stopped crying, she sent me back to my room to calm down and wash my face. When I came back down a few minutes later, walking this time, everyone was in the dining room, eating breakfast. I sat down and ate in silence for a few minutes. I could sense that everyone was worried, so I said, "The master chief really has that down good, doesn't she?" The girls smiled. "I think that we should rent her out." Betsy was coming close to losing it, so I added, "I think we should consider renting her to the president to get Congress in line."

Betsy nearly spit her food out, she was laughing so hard.

When she finally calmed down, she said, "Freddy, you did that on purpose."

"The sad emotions were getting too thick in here."

Melanie looked horrified. "How can you let her get away with that?"

"Melanie, I can feel the love she has for me, so I understand that it's her way to handle these things, and it works for the team. They don't do anything that would cause her to get mad. When they heard me get chewed out the first time and saw that I took it, that's when I was considered part of the team. The girls treated me a lot differently after that because then, I fit in. I was one of them, part of their fraternity. Besides, I deserved it. The master chief has told me before about not doing that, but all I could think about at that moment was breakfast, and I forgot. It was my fault, and I deserved the punishment. If I didn't deserve it, I would still take it, but when she calmed down I would let her know. So far, every time she's ripped on me, I've deserved it."

"Yes, you have." The master chief had entered the room. "I don't see treating any member of this team any different from the rest. If I have to do that, then that person is not a part of the team. Freddy knows that even in an emergency, he has to obey, just like the rest, and we don't have time for questions. So when I holler, everyone jumps. It's the way it has to be. We can talk about it later and decide if I was right or wrong, but at the moment I tell you to jump, you had better jump."

The admiral added, "Quick-response training has proven to be the best and most highly effective training for all military functions, all ship functions, and all situations where there is a command structure. Police, firefighters, and emergency rescue teams—everyone uses it except the government." He looked at the president. "It would run better if people would stop debating everything and just do what's right. It's nice to see that Freddy is willing and able to handle the training. It says a lot for the lad." Both generals had to agree. The talk around the table was light and easy after that.

The president asked, "Is everything ready to go inside, Freddy?"

I looked at Susan, who said, "I'll answer that."

The president exclaimed, "Oh, sorry! I keep forgetting that you're in charge. Actually—and please don't take offense, Freddy—I find it less frightening to know that the commander is governing everything and that you're willing to be governed."

I looked at her and said most sincerely, "So do I." That made her relax even more.

Susan said, "We know that you're a very busy person, so we worked until after midnight to get everything ready. We can go in right after breakfast. We'll be taking everyone in with us."

I looked at her with surprise and hoped I looked just a little upset. I pathed to Melanie and Katie, *"Don't let on, please."* Then, out loud, I said, "I thought we talked about this!"

"We did, and I said I'd think about what you said last night. I thought about it and have made my decision. I would like everyone to see what you're doing. I need the team to understand the enormity of the job you've taken on and why you're so tired all the time. I need the admiral and the president to see what you've done so that they know what they need to do. The civilians need to help so they should see. The generals are the only ones who won't be going in."

"You can't … please don't do this!" I begged.

"I have decided to give the generals the cube." She said "the cube" quietly and with great respect, as if it were the most priceless thing in the world—and she might have been right.

I started crying a little. Just enough to let everyone know something major was up. "Please, Susan, don't give them that information. How can you trust them? These are the most important discoveries since ... since ... well, ever. They make my little toys look like little toys. Information is power, Susan. This will give them great power."

"Wait!" the president said. "What are you two talking about?"

"Tell her, Freddy," Susan ordered.

I looked down at the table and kept my head down, looking as humble as I could as I pulled the cube from my pocket. "I wanted to test some of my toys," I said, pouting. "That's the FTL—faster-than-light—drives, the FTL communication, and special sensors, so I built one hundred probes. I sent them out five months ago at 250 times the speed of light. They've been sending me information ever since. There are over 157 billion gigabytes of information on space, solar systems, habitable planets, and other life forms, including intelligent life, all on this one cube. I told the commander last night that with everything else I've had to do lately, I just don't have time to look at it, but I have the feeling it's real important."

I could hear the intake of breath all around. Melanie looked at the president and said, "Breathe, Madam President, breathe."

She let out a breath and asked, "Freddy, do you know if there are habitable planets out there?"

"I only saw a small fraction of the information, so I only know of three. Two are like Earth, and one is better, I think. But I'm not a specialist in these things. Lots of vegetation and animals, if that means anything. I didn't look any further, as I have a lot of other work to do. I simply don't have time.

To give this information to the army is asking a lot. They would need to study it, get expert opinions, and have press conferences about their findings and all kinds of things."

I could feel the generals' eagerness.

The commander pressed in. "Madam President, I think this information is extremely important and needs to be looked at and studied right now. The navy is going to be too busy learning to fly Freddy's ships. The army has all the connections to pull this off, and they're under your thumb. They know what data to reveal and what to keep secret, and they'll be the ground crews when we start to explore new planets. I think the army is the best choice."

"I agree," said the president.

"I don't!" I said.

General Tankman said, "Look, Freddy, try just this once to trust us. We won't let you down. You have my word."

The commander said, "Freddy, I want the generals to take that cube and a player right now and get on the helicopter. They need to get started." She reached over and whispered to General Tankman, "Before I lose control over him."

I picked up the cube, and, with a tear in my eye, I set it in the commander's hand. "Make sure they only let the media that's cooperating with my lawyers have any information."

She gave the cube to the generals, and they immediately said their good-byes. The president said, "I want reports daily."

"Yes, Madam President." They turned and left. The president told the flight crew that she'd get a different ride home.

It was only a matter of minutes before they were gone. As soon as they were outside the shield, the admiral asked, "I know what you pulled in there, Commander. But are you sure that was a good idea?"

"Ask me that after you see what Freddy's been building in his shop."

He said, "I need a phone. I'll need to get a ride from Admiral Bates to get the president home."

I said happily, "Not to worry. We'll take her home in one of the shuttles. As long as we treat it like a plane, then no one should care. Right, Susan?"

"Right, Freddy. It will actually give us some productive flight time in the real thing. Petty Officer Smith will get us flight clearance to Washington, DC, and back. We'll set you down right on the White House lawn. Right, Freddy?"

"Right. We'll have you there in about ten minutes after takeoff. Right, Susan?"

"Wrong. Petty Officer Smith, you set it up for military high-level flight at eighty thousand feet, and we'll run her up to two thousand miles an hour, max. I don't want too many questions."

"Sorry," I said.

"That's okay, Freddy."

I looked at the president and said, "See? That's why she's the boss."

✦

Gray took hold of his weapons so hard that all the color was forced from his hands, and his face was scrunched in nearly a growl. He was furious and said, "He tricked those generals."

Everything went black after a few seconds of tickling. *"Not fair!"*

Yellows said, "The mistrust in the army is well founded. You can read the reports later. His trust in the navy is remarkable."

Blue added, "This president seems different from our royalty. I would like to know more about her."

Green said, "I will cut a crystal for you tonight."

Blue said, "Thank you."

Yellows said, "Another interesting thing—how much is a gigabyte of information?"

Green answered, "If I understand correctly, then 157 billion gigabytes is 157×10^{18} power."

Yellows asked, "How much does one of our crystals hold?"

"Less. Much less."

Blue said accusingly to Green, "Another bit of technology we could use. Amazing how some young systems can come up with inventions we cannot. Please continue."

CHAPTER 18

✦ ✦ ✦

HEALING A FRIEND

After breakfast, I asked, "Madam President, can we talk, just you, Melanie, Susan, and me, please? It will only take a minute."

She looked at the admiral. "I guess so."

I said, "Admiral, this is about girl stuff. It has nothing to do with my project. Okay?"

He laughed. "No problem, Freddy. I understand. I'd still like to talk to Admiral Bates."

The commander took control and sent the admiral away with one of the girls. I took the president, the commander, and Melanie into the commander's office. I pulled the curtains closed and turned to the women. "Melanie, you're thinking out loud, and you're doing it on purpose."

Melanie said, "I'm worried about her, and she won't ask you herself."

The president started to say something, but I raised my hand for her silence and asked Melanie, "Why?"

"She doesn't want to impose on you."

I put my fists on my hips, and, mimicking my mother, I said, "Oh, for goodness sakes. How childish! Madam President, you came here to impose on me, to get me to work on a world crisis, but you can't ask me for a simple favor that would take little or no time?"

"I thought I was already asking enough of you. I didn't want to take advantage of our friendship."

"What's friendship for if you can't push on it a little? I'll be asking you for favors sometime, and I won't hesitate. I may send the commander to ask, if I think you'll get mad at me." I looked at Susan with a sly grin. "But I'll still ask. The worst you can say is no. And the worst I can say is no, so what do you need?"

She straightened up, showing her good upbringing, and with shoulders erect, she asked, "Freddy, will you please heal me?"

"No!"

Everyone's mouth dropped open in incredulous disbelief. I started laughing. Susan smiled, and so did Melanie.

Melanie said, "Madam President, he's kidding. He fully intends to heal you. I think he would whether you asked or not."

I calmed down enough to blurt out between snickers, "You should have seen your face, Susan. I got you that time." Even the president was smiling now. Laughter can be catchy.

Susan said, "I'm sorry, Madam President. Freddy's sense of humor can be really off the wall at times."

"I see," she said, with just enough reproach in her tone to sober me up fairly quick.

Still smiling, I placed my hand on her cheek and closed my eyes. I stopped smiling. "You have breast cancer, and it has spread to the lymph nodes. There is some in your bones too. A little has broken off and is anchored in your brain and has started to grow. It will cut off the blood flow in that vessel soon, and you will have a stroke. You also have a corn." I was genuinely surprised and said, "I didn't think the president was allowed to have corns."

She smiled at me. "I wish, but it seems that we're still human, Freddy."

"Okay, so let's get this completed before the admiral gets worried. Do you want anyone to leave? I need to have you undress." She looked at me with big eyes. "Oh, don't give me that kind of look. Think of me as your doctor. Besides, I've seen it hundreds of times. When the girls first came here, I took all the peeks I could get. I think they knew, but they let me get away with it. After a while, the novelty wore off. Now, I think they look better with their clothes on. It's no big thing, now that I know exactly what they're hiding under there."

She said, "No, they can stay." She started getting undressed.

"Please leave your panties on and your stockings, as I don't need to touch that area."

"Thank you."

I talked to Susan about who would fly the shuttle tonight. I was trying to get the president to relax by acting like I wasn't interested, that this was nothing, and it seemed to be working. Susan knew what I was doing and went along with it. When the president was ready, I nonchalantly walked over and placed my hands, which I had been keeping in my pockets to warm them up, on the parts of her body that I needed to fix. It only took a few seconds at each spot, and then I said, "All done. You can get dressed now … and thanks."

"Thanks?" she asked.

I looked in her eyes. "Yes, thanks. Thanks for allowing me to heal you. This is not a good time to have you dying on us. I love you, and besides, I don't want to have to deal with someone else."

She got dressed while Melanie, Susan, and I talked shop. Melanie was very interested in how I could heal. The president had tears in her eyes the whole time we were talking. When she was finished dressing, she came over to me, got down on her knees to be at my level, and then gave me a big hug, saying, "Thank you, Freddy. I love you too."

I hugged her back. When she calmed down, we left the office and picked up all the girls, except the one on watch, and headed toward the shop.

✦

"Green!" Yellows bellowed.

Green jumped. That was a weird feeling—a tentacle jumping around in my head.

Everything went black, totally. I don't like being tickled. Besides, I was working out something else.

Green said, "Yes, Truth Taker."

Yellows said, "If you find out nothing else, you are to find out how he is doing this healing."

Green smiled. "I already know, Truth Taker. It is very complicated, and it will be in my reports."

Blue asked, "Is there a chance that we can learn this wonderful ability?"

Green said, nearly under his breath, acting like he was about to get yelled at again, "No, sire. We have not evolved to that stage yet."

All eyes were on me again, and they were astounded. Yellows said with threat in their voice, "Green, are you saying that this creature is higher in the evolutionary scale than we are?"

"No, Truth Taker. They are far behind us on the

evolutionary scale. They are simply evolving in a different direction. I can only guess as to what they will become."

"*I got it. I can't play with Yellows, as she, he, it—whatever—is too focused on keeping me unfocused. However, Green is not, and we have tactile contact. Let's keep this a secret for now.*"

Yellows said, "Very well. We look forward to reading your report. Continue."

CHAPTER 19

✦ ✦ ✦

NEVER UPSET A MASTER CHIEF TWICE IN ONE DAY

At the shop entrance I asked, "Everyone ready?" What the commander did not know was after she went to bed last night, I had teleported back to the shop and set up a few surprises.

Petty Officer Henderson said, "We're ready, Freddy." Several of the girls laughed.

I smiled at her, saying, "You be careful in there, Patricia. We all know how helpless you females can be." Laughter spread out across the group. "Shop?"

"*Yes, Freddy?*"

"Open up fully. I'm going to take everyone on a tour."

"*Password, please?*"

"Excuse me?" I said with feigned surprise. "What password?"

"*The one that was set using your codes last night from a remote area south of here.*"

"Did you monitor the person who set the password?" I asked.

"*Yes.*"

"Who was it?"

"*General Tankman.*"

"What password did he use?"

"*I am not allowed to say.*"

"Thank you. Well, that's just wonderful."

The commander asked, "Is there any other way in?"

Betsy, our resident expert in escaping out of or into anyplace, said, "Not a chance."

"Shop?"

"*Yes, Freddy?*"

"At what level are the defenses set?"

"*1-A1.*"

"Please change the level to 1-A2."

"*Password, please?*"

"Shop, override all passwords, code 234AD3."

"*Password, please?*"

"Sorry, Shop. Thank you. There's no way in. I can't reproduce the equipment or the bombs in time. We're dead without that password."

The admiral became upset and said, "I'll flay the skin off them until they talk. I'll ram that bastard in a tube and suck the atmosphere out slowly until he implodes. I'll—"

I couldn't hold it in any longer. I was rolling on the ground with laughter, and so were the girls—after they realized what I had pulled. Even the president was amused, but the master chief was not, and neither was the admiral.

"Freddy," said the master chief, "I think we need to have a private conversation." She took my arm and led me off, saying, "We'll be right back."

I think the whole assembly could hear my screams. I teleported off her lap when she was done spanking me. I was not stupid enough to do so while she was punishing me because that could cause her to lose count, and she would have to start all over. It took a few moments to get myself together before heading back out.

When I got back to the group, each girl I passed reached down and patted my behind. "Ouch! Stop that! Ouch! Ouch!" I finally got to the door. "Shop?"

"Yes, Freddy?" it answered with an amused tone.

"Please disconnect and discontinue," I said, interspersing my words with sniffles, "all the things we planned last night under code funny."

"Good idea, considering the master chief's mood right now, Freddy. I have disconnected all eighteen traps."

After she heard "eighteen traps," I heard the commander tell the master chief, "Good job. Thank you."

✦

Gray was smiling from ear to ear. "I like this creature."

All others just stared at Gray incredulously.

Everything stayed completely in focus. Strange sight these creatures have. I was using Green's eyes to see and his mind to turn the knob down again. The Green watching the knob had gotten busy on something else and left it unattended. Bad Green. Shame on it.

Yellows said, "We personally do not like having jokes played on us or anyone else."

Blue raised a tentacle, confirming it felt the same.

Gray said, "Loosen up a little. The creature is normally boring. That was more entertaining."

"Boring!" Using Green's mind, I mentally turned the switch off and took one of Gray's tentacles and slapped the little Yellows in the head. Pandemonium broke loose.

All were yelling at one another. At the same time, little Yellows dropped me and grabbed Gray, throwing him across the room and into several other Grays. I drifted down.

Blue tried to grab me but pulled me in the wrong direction, while Green was trying to snatch me the other way. I turned around, put a hand out, and touched the side of the tank. They went into shock. The bigger Yellows nearly screamed at the little Yellows. Five Grays were seriously injured, and the little guy picked up three more. For the smallest in the room, little Yellows were devastating. I smiled at the Green and Blue, and that panicked them even more, and they dropped me.

Something else came into the room. Something dark and foreboding said one quiet word: "Stop."

Everything came to a complete stop. Even little Yellows stopped.

Green turned to the new creature, and it was black as night. It was difficult to see and hard to watch. When it moved, it distorted. The new creature said to little Yellows, "Put them down, and resume your place."

Little Yellows gently set the three Grays down and came to the tank, lifted me up, and held me in the center.

It turned to the bigger Yellow. "You are in charge. What went wrong here?"

"Dark One, Gray slapped my pen mate in the head for no reason. She took great offense and threw Gray against his pen mates and then started tearing them apart. I was just about to join her."

Black said, "You are wrong. Let me tell you what happened. I have been tapped into the creature for some time. The creature took offense at being called boring by Gray, and so it used Green's mind to turn off the switch and then to cause Gray to hit your pen mate."

They all looked at me, upset. Black continued. "The creature is not at fault. It is simply trying to slow you down and is being very successful. Still, it is limited with the tank power on, so it finds ways to turn it off. This would not have happened if that Green had done his job and watched the power switch to this tank. He did not."

A tentacle shot out and touched the Green. It died instantly and in great pain. Another tentacle motioned toward another Green. "Turn that knob up full, and watch it very closely."

Black turned to Yellows and said very nicely, "Do not make me come in here again." It turned to me and said, "Creature, do not cry over that dead Green. He made a mistake that I had noticed earlier and would have punished anyway." Then it turned in a blur and left.

Not a word was said. The Green motioned for two Purples to remove the dead Green and for Green to continue.

Green said, "I will try, but it is hard while the creature is in such an emotional state."

Yellows asked, "This creature is sad over the death of one of ours?"

"Very."

Yellows motioned for the Grays to take away their injured. "Interesting. Please try to continue."

✦ ✦ ✦

CHAPTER 20

THE PARKING LOT

"Shop, please open the door," I said with a sniff.

Betsy patted my behind again saying, "Eighteen!"

"Ouch! Quickly, Shop!"

The door opened, and I swear I could hear the shop computer laughing very low. We entered the office area. Everyone looked around, but there was nothing to see here.

I handed the commander a list and asked through my sniffling, "What communication device would you suggest for each person?"

She read it, with the master chief looking over her shoulder.

Dot clear: master communication only.

Dot yellow: one warning and master communication.

Dot green: one warning and a report to a master and communication.

Dot red: continues to warn and report to a master and communication.

Dot blue: continues to warn. If warning is not heeded, it disintegrates and then reports to communication.

Dot black: No warning. Do something it doesn't like, and it disintegrates and then reports to communication.

"Shop, please upgrade the commander to security class 1-A2," I instructed, still unable to stop sniffling.

Everyone looked up. The commander said, "Thank you, Freddy."

"No problem. You deserve it," I said, sniffling in between every few words. "Now you can get Shop to do things for you." I sniffled again.

The master chief asked, "Are these dots necessary? Stop that sniffling!"

The commander said, "Yes, they are."

Colleen added, "The sniffling is a chemical thing that can't be stopped easily. He's already calming down, and I'm sure it will stop soon."

"Shop?"

"*Yes, Susan? Nice to have you in control. May I report to you when I think Freddy is getting close to killing himself again? I'm afraid he does it quite often.*"

Her eyes widened. "Yes, I would very much like to know." She gave me a "we'll stop that right now" look that the president and everyone else mimicked quite well.

"Please supply me with a yellow dot, and the rest of the team with green dots, and red dots for the admiral, the president, and our civilian guests. Freddy already has a clear dot, correct?"

"*Yes.*"

"Thank you. Please change his to a yellow dot, and have all dots report to me."

"Give me a break, Commander. It's my shop," I whined.

"Yes, and the computer just told on you. I won't have you getting yourself in trouble. Got that?"

"Yes, ma'am," I answered humbly. I couldn't see the dot, but by the looks everyone was getting, including me, I knew a yellow dot was near my right ear. The commander showed them how they were handled and how to communicate with them.

"Shop?"

"*Yes, Freddy?*"

"Report all emergencies to both the commander and me, and report all issues with the commander to my unit."

"*Completed.*"

I smiled up at Susan. "Someone has to cover you."

"That's right, Freddy, and thanks." She raised her voice. "Time to see the main workshop. Shop, please open the doors between here and the construction area."

"*Completed.*"

"Thank you. Let's go," she said.

We traveled down the hall. I brought up the rear so that the girls couldn't smack my behind anymore. The door to the construction area was eighteen feet high and forty feet wide. It looked tiny compared to what lay on the other side.

When I caught up with the group, they were all staring at the view. I let Susan guide them. "To our left is the destroyer. We'll be going through it in just a few minutes. Over to the right is Freddy's building-mover ship. It's still in the early stages of assembly, but as you can see, it will be big enough to move some very large buildings."

Dr. Landers said, "He's serious."

Most the team looked at him. Colleen asked, "What did you think? That he's been working himself to death building paper airplanes?"

"I never imagined … I mean … who could have thought a child could do so much? It would take NASA a decade to build a ship this size."

The president said, "It would take NASA that long just

to decide who was going to work on the project. We need to change all that. Ladies and gentlemen, the government is no longer the leader in space; a little boy is." She put an arm across my shoulders. "Aren't we ashamed?"

"Ashamed or not," said Astronaut Williams, "I can tell you this. Almost everyone I know at NASA and throughout the world will want a job with Freddy. The moment this gets out, there won't be enough jails to arrest all the people who will flock here. And the US Postal Service is going to be swamped." He smiled at the commander. "You're going to need your own postal branch."

I looked up at the commander with a worried look. "Is that true, Susan?"

"Don't you worry about a thing," she said. "We can handle it. If it comes to that, you will never see it. The team will take care of everything."

The admiral added, "Nothing is going to take you away from your playtime unless you want it to."

I smiled and said, "Okay."

Betsy said, "Freddy's taken playing spaceman to a new level, don't you think?"

Everyone laughed. I looked at her and mouthed, "*Thank you.*" She winked at me. The girls knew how much I liked it when everyone was happy.

The commander continued. "Over there"—she pointed to the far wall—"is where Freddy stores the little ships. As you can see by the number completed, Freddy's been very busy."

Lieutenant Bergman looked down and asked me, "How fast are these ships?"

"I'm not sure, Lieutenant. They're much faster than the probes, and the bigger the engines, the more powerful they are. If you compare them with the standard set by *Star Trek* writers, I would guess that the shuttles could achieve speeds exceeding warp seven, the fighters warp eight, and the destroyer can hit warp 9.5—it has very big engines. For some reason, the writers did not think traveling faster than that was possible—perhaps for the show; I have no idea. However, I have ideas that could make traveling between galaxies possible and nearly instantaneous. I have a long way to go before I start developing that, though. Besides, we've a perfectly good galaxy to explore right here."

"I'm sorry, but I don't understand warp speed," said the president.

Marian said, "Warp speed is based on multiples of the speed of light. Warp one is one times the speed of light, and warp nine is approximately 1,516 times the speed of light. That means the destroyer can travel to the next star in about one day. In a month, you can check out thirty solar systems. Freddy's probes have been traveling for five months at 250 times the speed of light, or just a little faster than warp four. If you say that stars are separated by about five light-years on average, then each probe has seen somewhere around sixteen solar systems. He sent out one hundred probes, which would mean we just gave the army the information on 1,600 solar systems."

"My ships don't have warp drives. It's something completely different," I said. "They don't bend space, and they don't change or pass through other dimensions." With a thoughtful expression, I said, "I could do that, I suppose." Then I shook my head. "But the dangers are not worth the advantages at this time. We have too much to look at close up within our own galaxy. Taking into consideration that the probes travel almost in a straight line from solar system to solar system, and they don't have human input, I would say that probably several have crashed by now. Shop?"

"*Yes, Freddy?*"

"How many probes are still sending?"

"*Ninety-seven.*"

"Hey, that's really good. I was expecting much fewer. This is great! That means that we have good maps with good routes to other systems. Shop, look on my to-do list, and check off mapping nearby solar systems."

"Completed. You now have 1,785,693 jobs left."

I cringed and said, "I may not get that vacation after all."

The commander looked at me and said, "Yes, you will. If I have to have the team drag you away, you're going to take a rest. Shop, do we know why the three stopped sending?"

"Yes. One crashed into an asteroid belt, one ran into a black hole, and one was shot down."

"Shot down?" the admiral said. "That's not good."

"You had to expect that there was intelligent life out there somewhere," said the president.

"Yes, but we're talking intelligent life with the ability to shoot down a probe traveling at warp four. The probe had shields and was not harming anyone, which means it was an act of aggression. That means that there is an aggressive life form out there with the ability to reach us within five months—and they know we're here."

The commander said, "This is a topic we can debate for months. What we're here to do is look at the ships that will be traveling with us to destroy that 'rock' and then get out of Freddy's way. Let's continue."

As we walked toward the destroyer, I said, "Admiral?"

"Yes, Freddy?"

"With this new information, I think I need to change my priorities a little."

"What do you mean? Destroying that rock is the top priority."

"Yes, but within that project is learning to use the equipment. I don't think we have time for little games on the trainer anymore. With the commander's permission, I think we need to put up a few ships now."

The commander said, "I agree. If we could have several of the smaller ships, we could get the knowledge and feel of the crafts quicker. We could play against each other and get a good understanding of how they work. I think the girls can teach the others very quickly. How many ships can you give us now?"

"It's not just that, Susan. They haven't been tested. I may need to redesign some things because, after all, I'm not a pilot. I built these on input from the girls' using the trainer."

"Good point. How many, Freddy?"

"I can give you forty Stingers, eighteen Sting Rays, nine shuttles, and possibly two specials."

The commander looked at me and asked, "Two specials? You've shown me everything except those. Where are you keeping them, and where are the other ships? You don't have nearly that many here."

I looked down, and, sounding quite guilty, I said, "In the parking lot. These are here because my parking lot is full. I made a mistake on the amount of space I needed. The specials are six-person ships. They're almost all weapons, shields, and engines. They were made to do several things. They're long-distance watch ships, built to report, catch, and destroy. The weapons can destroy cities or bounce a balloon back and forth between them. Each one can easily take on our visitors' largest ship. In the wrong hands and without the other ships I have to protect us, they could terrorize the world, and no one could do anything about it—except possibly me. I wasn't planning on giving them out."

"Why do you call them specials?"

"I haven't thought of a name or a category for them. I thought maybe a shark, but that would be downplaying them. They really are gunships."

✦

Gray said, "Gunships!"

Everything went black after the tickling.

Gray continued. "Disasters, more like it. Those little ships are mean, fast, and darn hard to hit. I lose, on average, six ships for every one of his gunships. We won't even talk about his blink ships. We haven't figured o—" He looked around as if being watched and quickly motioned for Green to continue.

C H A P T E R   2 1

✦ ✦ ✦

GIVING OVER RESPONSIBILITY

"Freddy, everything you've made so far, except the shuttles and the mover ship, has had weapons. Why?" asked the president. "You flat out refused to build such things for us before."

I looked at her accusingly and said, "The ideas that your generals had for my abilities had nothing to do with the protection of the world. They wanted advantage over the rest of the world. Sure, my inventions would provide that, but this is not what I wanted to build. Knowing that rock is up there has changed my intentions, and the generals messing with my home and my friends caused me to think that I needed protection for my protection. I built the fighters to protect my shuttles, and I built the Sting Rays to protect the destroyer. I built the gunships to protect the solar system from our visitors before I knew they were friends, and if it weren't for that rock and the generals, I'd be sitting on the moon right now."

"I'm sorry, Freddy. I know you don't want to have to build or use this stuff."

"It's so hard. I didn't want to build this kind of thing, but if I didn't, I would be the only one alive in two years. That would be a bad thing. I'm so afraid of building them, of what they can do in the wrong hands, and of who should have them that I cry myself to work almost every day. I built this many so that if someone bad gets one, then I can give the others to the navy for protection. Now, with this information, I need to give everything to the navy." I smiled. "It's a really good thing that the commander and my family are here." I gestured to show I meant the girls. "They won my trust, or you wouldn't get anything."

The commander put her hand on my shoulder and lovingly squeezed. "We're very glad you care enough about the human race and us to work on protecting us, but here again, that's supposed to be our job, and you're stepping over the line. It's my job to step over the line. Remember the talk we had?"

I nodded my head.

Susan continued. "You invent and build, but I take the responsibility. The job of ensuring that the ships are only in the best of hands is mine. People who feel the same way you and I do will be the ones who will fly those machines."

"I'll gladly give you the responsibility because I don't want it," I said, hugging her. "Remember, though, I need to patent this stuff. Shop, how far behind am I on patents?"

"According to your murmuring during your design-and-build phase, I would estimate that you have approximately 8,527 items that you need to patent."

I looked at Susan pleadingly, and she laughed, saying, "I'll find someone to help with the paperwork. You finish that destroyer."

We took a skid to the other side of the build area, and I ordered Shop to open the inside doors to the hangar bay. Betsy saw a big black spot on the wall by the entrance and asked, "What's that?"

"Oh, just a little mistake I made."

"Actually, he blew himself up and was lucky to still be conscious enough to heal himself. He lay here for two days afterward, too tired to move."

"You know, Shop, I can reprogram you."

"Understood."

"Shop," Susan interjected, "Freddy will not reprogram you, and I want to know when something like that happens again. Understood?"

"Understood."

Susan looked at me and said, "Understood, young man?"

"Understood."

We went into the parking lot. Some of the girls were already looking at the ships, climbing into them, and checking out the controls.

One yelled down, "These controls are just like the ones on the trainer."

Another added, "Hey, these are too. I could fly this thing right now."

Captain Williams looked down from one of the gunships and whistled really loud. "This thing is loaded! There're controls for everything—weapons, navigation, science with environmental, sleeping quarters, restrooms, room for supplies, two fighters … and is this a kitchen? My God, it is! Everything's here to fly this baby now."

I looked up and said, "Dot, please tell the captain that it still needs to be provisioned, and tell him not to take the Lord's name in vain in my presence."

He looked out the hatch, said "Sorry," and then went back in.

The president smiled and said, "I didn't know that you believe in God."

"Of course I believe in God and Jesus Christ and the Holy Ghost. Don't you?"

"Yes, I do."

"Did you know that they're actually three separate beings?" I asked. "You really wouldn't think so, the way they do and say the exact same thing, but they are different. God, the Father, is really quite serious all the time—the God of this world. Jesus, the Son of the big God, gets amused over simple things and likes to be happy. The Holy Ghost has no personality at all—just tells you when you're about to mess up, which is more often than you'd think. I believe he still needs time on the planet. He doesn't have a body yet."

The president looked at me with a smile and changed the subject. "When can we have these ships, Freddy?"

"Why ask me? They're ready to go, so I've done my part. Ask the commander. She's in charge."

"You're going to stick to that deal?"

"Oh yes. If she gives these things away to the wrong person, then it's on her head, not mine. You can't imagine the weight that lifts from me. Madam President, I have a lot of work to do, so please come get me when you guys are ready to leave." I gave her a hug and said, "See you later."

She said, "Okay, Freddy."

I headed back into the workshop and into the destroyer.

The commander watched me go and then turned to the president. "You can't imagine the weight I just received."

"Yes, I can because I'm just as responsible as you. It's my people who will be flying these ships, and I'm responsible to you. We have to do a good job on this one, Susan. I'd hate to see what he has that will bring these down. Does it worry you that he has that kind of power?"

"He did say he could stop them, but no, I am not worried.

It makes me glad to know that his morals are well founded and that I don't have to worry about him. Let's look at him as a safeguard. If something goes wrong, then we have him to fall back on."

"I'm worried that our future hope is going out on that destroyer."

"I am too, Madam President. But there's not much choice on that. He's the only one who can repair anything that goes wrong, and if we don't make it, then the world is doomed."

"We?"

"I go where Freddy goes, and so does the team. There's plenty of room for the crews and the team but not much room for ride-alongs, so the scientists will have to wait until we get back before they go on any joy rides. Let's just concentrate on our jobs. What is it going to take to make this trip? It's a planning nightmare."

The admiral said, "Not really. I can give you all the needs and requirements in just hours. This is no different than deploying a navy destroyer to sea for an extended period of time, but I need to know how long we are going to be gone."

"About three days, sir."

"Thanks, Freddy. Listening in?"

"Yes, sir."

"We know how many ships and the types we have. Any fuel requirements?"

"The ships are fully powered and ready to go. All ships have enough power to run for at least two years, even if they have to use maximum shields and power weapons."

"That helps a lot. Fuel normally takes up a lot of space. Do the restrooms need toilet paper?"

I giggled. "No, sir."

"Do we need to take water or oxygen supplies?"

"No, sir. The water and air are generated and recycled, and the destroyer has enough to supply all ships with both for years. I expect it will get a little stale after about eighteen months."

"So it's just food, then?"

"No food requirements. I have replicators installed and enough raw materials to feed twice the number of people who will be aboard for years. That reminds me—the recipes are rather limited. Susan, we need to get Cooky to help us plan a better menu. So far, all I've fed it has been her sandwiches. It requires samples, you know."

"Okay. We'll get on it."

"How do we clean clothes?"

"You put them into the washer, and they automatically get completely broken down into their basic materials and rebuilt, minus the dirt and body fluids. They even come back pressed and folded. Susan, haven't you noticed that I don't generate much in the way of laundry anymore, yet my clothes are always clean?"

"Yes. I've wondered about that."

"You may want to take spares, though. It was hard sneaking back into the house when my washer broke down and would not replicate."

Betsy said, "You were caught, and we had a great laugh. We just never told you."

I was quiet for a second.

"Freddy, you okay?"

"Yes, Commander. I'm just waiting for the blood to stop draining from my face."

She laughed.

The president said, "I need to come here more often. Not only am I astonished at every turn, but I also get entertained."

My dot warned me that Marian was about to start up a

ship, and two girls were near it. I started to say something, but I heard the commander jump in. "Marian, stop!"

"What's up, Commander? I just wanted to see it start up. I wasn't going to fly it."

"Look under your ship."

"Uh-oh."

"Next time, heed that warning the dot gives you, or you're out of here. People! We do everything safe at this base. Got it!" They all answered in the affirmative.

The admiral and several others were going through the destroyer and were almost finished when the president looked at her watch. "I would love to stay longer, but I do need to get back to Washington."

"All right. Everyone listen up," said the commander. "Lock down everything, and let's get out of here. We're going to take the president home. I want a crew standing tall, Master Chief. Freddy and I will be going too."

"They're on the way, Commander."

I said, "Commander, I almost forgot. We need a name for all these ships and one for the shuttle before we take off. Remember what Captain Crain said? It's bad luck not to name a ship."

"Understood," Susan said. "Did everyone hear that? We need a name for the shuttle. I'll take suggestions after this place is locked down."

"I'm on my way too, Susan," I said. By the time I made it to the office, everyone was filing out.

"Shop," said the commander.

"*Yes, Susan?*"

"Is anyone still inside?"

"*Just Freddy and you.*"

"Is there anything else we should know or be made aware of?"

"*No.*"

"Did anyone leave anything behind or modify anything?"

"*No, Susan. I was monitoring, as you requested, and nothing was attempted.*"

"Good. Please lock down, and go to full security."

"*Compliance.*"

We walked out, and I heard the system slam into place. Nothing would get in until Susan or I approved it.

✦

Gray asked, "Food replicators?"

Everything went black, except I was now looking through little Yellows' eyes, and they were letting me. Yes, they are a "she couple." Their idea was that if I was using them, they could monitor and limit. Good idea, as it was working. At least for now.

Green answered, "It is apparent that some of the equipment you have confiscated is for cleaning clothes, making food, and environmental. It is not all weapons, as you thought."

Gray said, "The creature also has great weapons and better shields than ours. You Greens have had it for months now. When are we going to find out anything?"

Green said, "As soon as we have information, you will have it." Green turned to Yellows. "The technology is completely different, and our research resources are limited on this ship. Food replicators would be a big breakthrough for us. It would allow for far longer trips."

Yellows said, "Understood. Please continue."

CHAPTER 22

✦ ✦ ✦

FIRST MANNED (OR WOMAN-ED) SHIP TO ACTUALLY FLY

We walked to the shuttles, and I took the security off the first one. A team of SEALs were standing by. The rest were looking a little disappointed, so I asked, "Saving the rest for next time, Master Chief?"

"We have enough people for two crews, and that's the second crew. They have the duty on the next flight." She looked at the commander and said, "I was hoping you and I could switch too."

"I think that's a good idea, Master Chief," the commander said, "but I can't afford the time, so you will probably have to share the duty with the lieutenant."

I could feel her happiness at this. I think she thought that she would be left out.

"Aye aye, Commander. Will do."

"What's her name, Master Chief?"

"She's *Air Force One* until the president disembarks. Then, since she's the first of the ships to actually carry the president, we'd like to call her *America's Pride*."

I said, "I like that. Who thought up that one?"

"Colleen did."

"Tell her thanks for me, and let her know that I want the team to figure out names for the rest of the ships. Try to give them names that fit a category. All shuttles need to be named something with either America or Pride in the name."

"Will do, Freddy."

We boarded, and everyone settled down. Marian Smith was at navigation, Betsy Donet had weapons and science, Katie Swanson had communications, and Denise Potter had systems and shields. Melanie was sitting next to the president, Susan was sitting in the middle at the captain's spot, and I sat next to her. The admiral and the civilians wanted to stay at the base for a while.

Susan said, "Smith, set a course for the White House."

"Captain, we have presidential priority all the way and clearance to land on the White House lawn any time within the next two hours."

"Very good, Swanson. Smith, I want to drop on the White House lawn in exactly 1.5 hours."

"Plotted and set in, Captain."

I looked over at the president and said, "I think they watch too much TV."

The front screens came up, with a small insert at the bottom of the screen showing the sides and back. The shields came up, and I heard Katie ask the base for permission to depart.

"Permission granted. The shield door is open, and everything is clear up to ten miles. Good luck, friends."

"Thanks. Captain, we have clearance from home base for takeoff."

"Engage, and make me proud, girls." The commander was close to tears.

I reached out and touched her shoulders. "Good job, Captain."

She smiled but kept her eyes on the screens.

Air Force One/America's Pride lifted up slowly and smoothly. They had practiced long and hard on this. Each one of them must have felt as if she had flown around the world a thousand times, but that was nothing compared to the real thing.

We drifted almost straight up, just going to the side enough to align with the door in the base shield, and then we ascended at an alarming rate.

It took only three seconds before Marian reported, "Captain, we're at eighty thousand feet." She pushed the controls forward, and we shot out like a bullet. There was no noise and only a little feeling of movement. Thank goodness I had set the dampening controls correctly.

"Captain," I said, "please, on the first flight of any ship, start out slowly. If I'd set the dampers wrong or not matched up the shield velocity modulators, then we'd be mush right now."

"My fault. Got that, Marian? Everyone?"

"Understood," they said in unison.

"I trust your work, Freddy. But it's nice to know that you believe you're human."

"Captain, now that you're going to get reports from Shop, you'll see just how human I am, and you can look back on this takeoff and thank God for the blessing he just granted all of us."

She looked at me with shock. I was sweating and with good reason. I had seen what the wrong settings did to an apple. There had been nothing left but sauce, not even seeds.

After things were going well, the captain turned to the president and apologized for her error in judgment.

The president said, "Do that again, and I'm going to need a change of clothes! Apology accepted, but please be careful."

"Yes, ma'am. Now, Freddy, please explain to me why we don't feel the pressure of acceleration."

"Oh, that's easy." I spent the next hour going through the math. When I start talking shop, I forget that others have no idea what I'm saying. It was an hour before the commander stopped me and said, "Could you please go back to the point where I lost you?"

"Sure. Where was that?"

"When you said that it has to do with tricircular molecular physics."

"But that was …" I blushed. "Sorry."

"That's okay." She turned to the president. "I did that to show you why he has to go with us on the destroyer."

"I get your point," she said. "I doubt anyone in the world could keep up with him."

I said, "Dorothy Pendelson's father, Professor Jim Pendelson at MIT, and his team could. He was the main reason I invented tricircular physics. Some of it came from his ideas."

The president said to Susan, "Didn't she say that her father wanted to visit?"

"Yes. Very much."

"If he and his team can pass the screening, then I want them at the base, learning."

I said, "After the mission. I'll have no one except the commander in my shop again until I get rid of those bombs."

"I understand, Freddy, but he could stay at the base and learn on the ships you bring out."

"I guess so, if the commander agrees."

"Sorry, Madam President, but I think that's a bad idea. Freddy doesn't have time to teach the professor much at this point, and his stuff is not patented yet. We need to keep the distractions down as much as possible, and I can just see what would happen when the professor got there.

Three days later, he and Freddy would still be deep in a mathematical discussion that had no chance of ever ending."

I put my hands on my hips and said with a little indignation, "And what's wrong with that?"

They both looked at me and said at the same time, "Everything."

The president said, "I see what you mean. I bow to your expertise."

"Thank you."

"Captain, we're almost above the White House," said Marian.

"Swanson, do we have communications with the White House yet?" Susan asked.

"Yes, ma'am. They're ready and waiting for our landing."

"Carry on, navigator."

They were all smiling. This group was so happy, they were almost giggly, and this made me very happy. I couldn't help it. This kind of emotion is very contagious for an empathic person. It was easy to see that Melanie was the same way.

Melanie pathed in almost childish laughter. *"Freddy, do you feel that?"*

"Of course I do. Fun, isn't it?"

"I've never felt like this before."

Katie pathed, *"You're empathic, then; so is Freddy. I'm not, but the joy is so thick in here that everyone feels it. Look at the smile on the president's face. She's beaming. It's not just that they're flying this ship for the first time, but this proves that the ship works. For the first time in months, the president is allowing herself to be happy … hopeful … and she's transmitting this to everyone."*

"She's not telepathic, Melanie," I added, *"and she doesn't receive emotions at all, but she transmits her emotions, and when she does, it affects everyone. You need to attune yourself to this,*

and let her know when she's doing it. Teach her to use it. It's a powerful weapon for her if she can learn to control it."

"I will."

"*Good girl,*" said Katie.

"Captain, landing in five, four, three, two ... we're down."

"Good job, team. Donet, scan for issues, and report."

"All appears clear, Captain."

"Stand by to open the hatch."

The girls gathered their weapons from the weapon storage locker. "Set on lowest stun setting. I don't want an incident that we can't reverse," said Susan.

I put my hand on Susan's arm. "I haven't tested them yet, ma'am."

"We have, Freddy, and we had to readjust them a little. The ones you left in the trainer were adjusted so that stun meant 'cooked well done.' At the lowest setting, it disables at a distance of about one hundred and twenty feet. Anything higher, and your target is toast or complete dust. In addition, they have a charge that lasts for seventy full power shots. We tested out what 'full power' means, Freddy." She looked right into my eyes. "If you would have used that stunner at the airport last year, you would have killed all those men and removed the building and several other buildings! We need to talk about limiting the power of this design."

I blushed.

She turned to the team and said, "If everyone is ready, then open the hatch, Potter."

Two of the girls preceded the captain and me down the open hatch. When they were in place, the president and Melanie came down. We shook hands and thanked her, and she returned the thanks, all formal like. The president walked up to the White House with new Special Service personnel, and we reentered the shuttle.

Susan said, "Job well done, team. Now let's go home."

We talked about many things on the way, including opinions on everything that had happened in the last two days. When we were almost home, we received a call from the president.

Katie said, "Captain, the president would like us to know that the generals have already found seven planets that look promising."

I said, "Ask her if there were any signs of intelligent life on them."

"She says yes, on two of them, possibly three."

"Tell her that they found only five and possibly four, then. But let her know that trade contacts may be a possibility."

"She says she understands, and a team will be established to determine what our proper conduct should be."

"Hold on to that connection, please." I sat there in thought. After a few minutes, I said, "Tell the president that I am sorry for holding her up, and put her on speaker."

"Hello, Freddy."

"Hello, ma'am. I was thinking it would be a mistake to believe that any contact with another species is going to be mundane. The possibility of our wiping them out or their wiping us out is very real when you think on the microorganism level. On your team, I would suggest that you include a microbiologist, medical specialists, military, and someone who can hold to some form of morality without getting fanatical about it. I believe that some people will not listen to reason on this subject. People are going to want to put their hands on everything, as that is our nature, and that may not be the best idea. Please add in a telepath, if you have one, with orders that the political and secondary agendas are to be reported and canceled out. I know you're good at this kind of stuff, but Congress is not the right group of people to set this up. Also, I think it would be a good idea to send out probes to monitor these planets. I'll make some up and send them out after this current project is finished, and I'm back from vacation."

"Good ideas all, Freddy. I'll take them into consideration. Thanks."

"That's all I can ask. I'm glad you're the kind of person who will listen. Thanks."

The captain stepped in. "Madam President?"

"Yes?"

"How many people can I take away from NASA? I don't mean *borrow* either. I mean take and keep. I want them to belong to us."

"As many as you want. If you want the whole group, they're yours. Just say the word. I'll contact them and let them know. By the way, Captain, your new rank will be waiting for you when you get home. Good night." She hung up before anyone could say a word.

✦

Gray said, "They did not limit those hand weapons."

Little Yellows warned me, "Only look and listen."

I answered back, "As you wish ... at this time."

They smiled.

Green said, "We have several of the hand weapons, thanks to the Grays. However, we cannot duplicate them at this time. We are working on it."

Yellows asked, "Where are you testing them?"

Green said, "We tried the gunnery range in this ship. That was a mistake."

Gray said, "I thought one of their ships blew that hole in the side of this ship."

Green cringed. "No, it was one of my pen mates. Now we use a maximum shielded room."

Yellows said, "We have a question."

Green said, "Go ahead."

"What is NASA?"

Green said, "That is one we know well. NASA is one of their entertainment groups."

Gray asked, "That does not make sense. Why would this Black, called Susan, want to have entertainers for this scientific research?"

Green said, "Experience. This Susan needs creatures with experience. We have found many references that NASA spends a lot of time in space, and that entertainers spend a lot of time spaced out."

Yellows said, "Oh, you may be right on this."

Little Yellows smiled. "We think you are wrong; otherwise, why is the creature laughing so hard he has tears?"

Blue, with a half-smile and questioning tilt of his head, looked at little Yellows in surprise and said, "Green, continue."

✦ ✦ ✦

CHAPTER 23

BE
PROFESSIONAL

When we set down on the platform at home, the entire crew was waiting for us. As the commander left the shuttle, I heard the snap of attention and the lieutenant saying, "Welcome back, Captain Susan James." She handed the newly appointed captain sealed orders in a large package.

As I departed the shuttle, I received a roaring cheer. They were happy with the first run of one of my ships, and I received handshakes and hugs from everyone. The captain was reading the orders and yelled, "Master Chief!"

She returned to the new captain and saluted with a smile. "Yes, my captain?"

"You're out of uniform, and so is the rest of the team! Is that any way to start your limited duty officer career, Lieutenant?"

"No, ma'am!"

"I want the ranks in order—now!"

"Troops fall in." The girls ran around like headless chickens and got into lines. The new lieutenant said, "Close interval, dress right, dress." The girls put their right hands on their hips, with right elbows sticking out, and moved so that their elbow touched the next girl. It was all rather fascinating. When they were all lined up, the new lieutenant said, "Ready, two." The hands and elbows snapped down in unison, like it was one sound, crisp and clear, and they faced forward.

The master chief, now lieutenant, came forward and addressed the captain, saying, "Troops standing by, ma'am."

"Very good, Lieutenant." She turned to the group. "First, let me congratulate you on doing a great job with the president and her visitors. What I'm about to tell you is one of the most enjoyable jobs a captain can have. Lieutenant Junior Grade Daphne Morgan, front and center. Congratulations, Lieutenant Morgan, on your promotion." She took out a set of bars and handed them to Daphne. They saluted each other. This went on through the entire team. It seems that when I was in my workshop, they had taken some kind of proficiency tests, and every one of them had passed with flying colors. The president then pulled some strings to ensure that everyone was promoted. I had no idea that the master chief had applied for rank as an officer. I didn't know she could. This was great, and everyone was happy. Instead of waiting for a specific period, this group was promoted immediately. Darnel, Henderson, Swanson, Donet, Peters, and McMasters received the rank of chief. I giggled, as I could just see them running around with feathers in their hair, wearing moccasins, and Henry Peters wearing a headdress and carrying a spear. Smith, Parks, and Potter made first-class petty officer, and Pendelson made second-class petty officer. The new lieutenant grumbled something about not being allowed to initiate chiefs anymore. I was puzzled about that, but I could ask later.

The captain said, "One more thing." She gave the

envelope a shake. "Everyone attached to our team for any part of last year has been awarded a navy achievement medal."

I must give them credit. With emotions running so high, I couldn't see how they could hold rank and not even smile. I could tell the difference between the SEALs and the two additions. Those two were smiling and fidgeting. The lieutenant saw this and went right up to them. They weren't smiling now; they were standing stock still.

"Master Chief—oh, sorry—Lieutenant! Take over." The captain quickly departed with a look of satisfaction on her face.

The lieutenant yelled, "Everyone, except YNC Henry Peters and PN2 Dorothy Pendelson, dismissed."

Two of the girls, Colleen and Betsy, came over to me and led me away, saying, "You don't want to hear this, and they don't need the witnesses. Witnesses will only make the"— she paused—"lieutenant worse."

"Tell me about it," I said, while rubbing my behind. They laughed, and we crossed the first bridge toward the house. I could already hear the yelling. I felt sorry for those two. They were not used to being in such a well-disciplined unit. That really was no excuse, though, as even I knew better. I put up my shields after I heard, "How dare you embarrass me in front of the captain like that? I can see you need special training. How about you remove the water from that river, and put it in the other one? On the run. Move it!"

"What do we use, Lieutenant?"

"I didn't give you permission to talk!" she yelled.

I knew the two were out of shape, but they were breathing heavily before they reached the first river. I looked at Betsy and said, "Please tell the lieutenant I am appalled at the condition those two are in. I would expect them to be able to run longer before being winded."

She smiled and said, "You realize what that will do, don't you?"

"Yes, I do. I expect to start training myself as soon as this first project is completed. I never want to be that out of shape. You cannot afford to be out of shape and be in space."

"Good for you, Freddy. You always need to take time for exercise."

"I expect to do just that. Besides, you girls promised to teach me self-defense."

"That's right, and we will, as soon as you're ready."

"I can defeat any one of the team right now, but I would like to be better."

Betsy looked at me and said, "Really? Try to hit me."

"What?"

"Try to hit me. You said you could defeat me right now, so prove it."

I raised my hand, walked up to her, and gently slapped her. Then I went back to Colleen, and we headed back toward the house. Colleen was looking over her shoulder all the time. When we were a few feet away, I raised my hand, and let her loose.

Betsy immediately took a side step, saying, "That's not fair."

When she caught up, I said, "The master chief—oops, I mean, the lieutenant—says that all's fair in hate and war. Has she ever been in love? She seems to have a bad attitude about the subject."

"Freddy," said Colleen, "the lieutenant is, well … uh … she doesn't like men." She said it like I would get really mad or something.

"I know. She's very professional about it, but you'd think she could find someone with the same feelings that she has who might calm her down a little."

They looked at each other and stopped. I took a step

before I realized they had stopped, and I had to turn around to talk to them. They both kneeled down to my level, like they do when they want my full attention.

Colleen asked, "You don't mind, Freddy? I mean … well, I thought that you would be very upset when you found out."

"Why?"

"You're very close to God, and I would think that he has a thing against that kind of behavior."

"If he does, then that's his thing." I looked at her with a frown and said, "I was not put on this earth to judge someone else. Being gay is not for me, as I am totally heterosexual, but it is also not for me to say how someone else should live. If the lieutenant wants to be homosexual, that's between her and God. If she wants to ask me if I think it's proper, then I'll tell her I don't know. The Bible is ambiguous on the subject, and I am not a prophet. God does not give me directions on how to run others' lives." I leaned in and quietly said in a secretive manner, "He does give me some directions on my projects, but I hope he never wants me to tell someone she's living her life wrong. Goodness, I'd feel so bad. I love the lieutenant, and I will support her as best as I can." I leaned back and asked in a normal tone, "Why do people judge me on how they think I will react? It's really not fair. I don't do that to other people."

Betsy reached out and pulled me to her, hugging me. "It just comes naturally for some people. You're one of the few who has this great ability to take people as they are, and that's very rare."

"Well, I'm not going to change just to be like everyone else. I like the way I am, and I don't like making anyone unhappy"—I thought for a second—"except the army generals. You know what?"

"What, dear?"

"Sometimes I'm wrong, and sometimes I'm right. I never know when I will be one or the other, and I have no idea if I'm right on this subject or not, and I don't really care, as it doesn't affect me or my projects. I do know that being wrong sometimes makes being right much better. It sure would be boring if I was wrong all the time or right all the time. Don't you think?"

"Yes, I do," Betsy agreed. She kissed me on the forehead and turned me around. We continued heading to the house.

I jumped around, yelling, "They're here!" Then I made a turn and ran off so suddenly that both were taken by surprise. They ran after me.

✦

I said to the little Yellows, "*I was wrong and got that Green killed.*" I turned sad, and Green had to stop.

Little Yellows said, "*Do not worry so much, creature. You do not understand what happens when we die. It is not so bad, and it was a quick death.*"

Blue asked Green, "Why did you stop?"

Green said, "The creature just started going into depression and was pulled out."

Little Yellows said out loud, "He—and it is a 'he'—is very sad that a Green died because of him."

Green said, "A Red would be."

Gray said, "So they have field promotions, just like we do. Interesting."

Green looked at Gray and said, "You are an unfeeling snobtherger."

Gray started to physically reach out, but Blue said, "Don't start, you two. Green, continue when you can."

CHAPTER 24

✦ ✦ ✦

MORE TO TRAIN ON

I stopped at the four big boxes that were sitting on the dock. Lieutenant Daphne Morgan was looking at them too. She said, "They came in about two hours ago. Admiral Briggs said that you'd been waiting for them but wouldn't tell us what they are. We scanned them, and they look like some sort of boats."

"Commander, please unpack these, but don't put them into the water yet. I'll be right back. You think we can get some of the girls to help us?"

Betsy said, "I'll get them."

"Great." I ran off toward the workshop. When I came back, the crates were completely removed, and my four boats were there on the skids that I had provided to the company to build them on. Behind me, on four more antigravity skids, were the parts to finish building them.

"Here you go, girls." I smiled and left to go back to the house.

"Freddy?"

I turned around and asked, "Yes?"

"What is all this?"

By this time most of the team was out there. I answered, "Two twenty-foot antigravity short boats, one thirty-foot long boat, and one hundred foot by fifty foot cargo boat. I designed them myself. The hulls are impermeable. They run on energy packs that will allow you to run for years. They can float up to about one thousand feet above any surface, and the engines on those skids are fast enough to allow you to get from here to town in just minutes. You should have the docking stations in town by now, so you have a place to pick up equipment or just to park and visit." I smiled a mischievous smile and said, "I don't have time to play around putting them together now, so it's up to you. Good luck!" I turned around, nearly bursting with laughter. They had wanted local transportation for a long time, and now they had it. The only thing was, they had to put it together. The key thing I wanted out of this was for them to see how I build things and how they can work on my equipment. I turned back to them again and said, "By the way, the tool box is in the first skid, and the instructions are with each unit."

I turned back around and headed to the house. It was dinnertime, and I was getting hungry. As I entered, the captain said, "Have something new for the girls to work on, do you?"

"Yes, ma'am. I need them to learn to build things using my tools and working with my techniques. I figure that after four boats like those"—I crooked a thumb, pointing outside—"they should have a good handle on the basics."

"I was wondering when you'd get around to that. Nice job," she said.

"Captain, I need them to finish the scenarios soon. I'll be ready to go in about two weeks. We can do a shakedown cruise around Pluto or something, but I need those crews."

The admiral came up and said, "I have one hundred and eighty top pilots and engineers coming to the navy base tomorrow for screening. We'll have those pilots and crews within two weeks and have them trained also. In addition, I have SEAL Team Five coming in to help guard this base while the captain and her team are guarding you out in space. I have over eight thousand volunteers from NASA wanting to work on the projects as soon as you're ready, and I have all the required cargo ordered and lined up for delivery. The cook has twenty-five new recipes loaded into that module you gave her, including meatloaf sandwiches, which I understand is your favorite."

"Yes!" I said with great enthusiasm. I could feel the cook's love for my appreciation of her work. I looked at the captain and said, "Looks like you have a lot of work ahead of you, screening all those people."

"Not really, Freddy. I'm going to screen the five psychiatrists, and they will screen the rest using your lie detectors. They will do a much better job than I ever could. Katie will talk with each one who passes the test."

I frowned. "That will be hard on Katie. If she starts having headaches, you stop her. I don't want her to burn out."

She looked at me with concern and said, "Katie said she could talk to you all day and not feel tired."

I smiled up at her and said, "She's talking to someone who's a telepath." Then I said directly into the captain's mind, *"Talking to and reading someone who is not telepathic is much harder and can really hurt."* I said aloud, "I have more power than she does, so I can do it all day if I really need to, but I wouldn't, as I'd develop a headache that would be a killer all night. Don't let her work more than one hour in two. Ten minutes on and ten off would be best, with a thirty-minute break every two hours. In addition, ensure that she has plenty of nuts and some kind of carbohydrate snack on hand."

"That's right; I forgot."

The admiral asked, "Nuts and carbohydrates?"

The captain said, "Freddy let us know that telepaths use up fat and carbohydrates very quickly when utilizing their abilities. It's one of their limiting factors. Katie is going to use it up very quickly. I'll talk to Cooky. Colleen cooked pasta for Freddy when we were moving his home, and it helped a lot."

"Interesting! Did anyone think to tell the president so that she could pass this information on to the children she's finding?"

I looked at the captain and she said, "I don't think we did, but I'll take care of it. When this project is over, I'd like to take a trip to see this school for the telepathically talented. I think Freddy can help them in a lot of ways. It won't take long."

Cooky came in and told us that dinner was ready. The captain sent one of the girls out to summon the rest.

✦

Gray said, "Did you catch that? They are limited in their powers by food intake."

Green said, "I will adjust the liquid to exclude fats and carbohydrates."

Yellows said, "No, you won't. If you take away his food, he will become sick and have a headache. Will you be able to pass through the headache and obtain information?"

Green said, "No. It would become very difficult."

Blue was watching and said, "Then continue."

✦ ✦ ✦

ES PROTECTRESS

The talk around the table was about the boats. All of the manuals I had printed were at the table being studied. The ones reading them paid no attention to any of the conversations. I started giggling.

"What's up, Freddy?" asked the lieutenant. She was the last one inside, and both of the new team members were still upstairs, trying to dry off. For some unknown reason, each had fallen in the river several times.

I said, "It's just that these four have teased me constantly about my concentrating on my work during meals, and now they're doing the same thing. Watch this. Patty," Then, a little louder, I said again, "Patty." No response. "Patricia." Still no response. Nearly yelling, I said, "Chief Patricia Henderson." No response whatsoever. I nearly fell out of my chair, laughing.

The admiral said, "Yes, but they're trained SEALs. Watch this." He whispered so low that I could hardly hear him. "Freddy's in ..." I raised my hand in fear and stopped his breath so he could not say the last word.

"Admiral!" said the lieutenant as she motioned for me to let him go. "Don't ever do that. They may kill someone." Everyone was glaring at him except those four. Then the lieutenant made a tiny motion with her hand, and all four pulled weapons that I had no idea they had and looked at the lieutenant for orders. She made another movement, and they went back to reading. "Yes, they're trained, but what you were about to say could have gotten everyone in this room killed if they were not on the team. I don't want to have to send letters to all these nice civilians' relatives." She turned to me and said, "Thanks, Freddy."

I looked at her with wide eyes. "Remember when I said something like that? I'll never forget it, and I'll never do it again. I had nightmares for a week."

"What happened?" asked Dr. Landers.

"Let's just say that if I had pulled that stunt in the middle of town, there would be no town."

"I've always thought that the military is too zealous, and that just proves it," the doctor said.

"I disagree," I said. "At first I thought they were … what's a good phrase? Oh yes, let's say extremely closed-minded. I thought that they would run my life and give me no choices in what I do."

He said, "Seems to me they're doing just that."

I could feel the girls getting mad. I knew that was a bad thing. "I think you're assessing them wrong, sir. Yes, they take their jobs very seriously, and that has saved my life several times. Yes, they seem fanatical about doing their jobs. In this situation, that is exactly what I need, but they also protect me from me. They teach me, watch over me, and make sure I have manners and that I don't use my abilities to the detriment of others. By the way, Admiral, I'm sorry for taking your breath away, even for a few seconds."

"It's all right, Freddy. You had a very good reason."

"Thanks. The girls never tell me what I can or can't do as far as work is concerned, and they would never even try to teach me about life if I didn't allow it. Earlier today, I received a good lesson from the lieutenant. There was a good reason for it, but if I told her not to touch me, she wouldn't. I own this base and can kick them all off in an instant."

"You really believe that?"

The captain said, "Freddy made an agreement with me that we can raise him properly so that he does not turn out spoiled, and we help him stay alive, for which he allows us to stay here. If he said, 'Team, pack up and leave,' then we would go. The president would be very upset with our team and would come here begging Freddy to allow us to come back, but we would do whatever he tells us to do. If he had said, 'Kill those generals and the president,' we would have done so instantly. Zealousness? It may seem to be, but those are our orders. If our orders were to be wishy-washy in our duties, we would be like civilians until our orders changed."

I think she said that as a slam to Dr. Landers. I continued. "So far, the team has treated me just like one of their own. They protect me, teach me, and help me, and I do the same for them. Can you imagine, Dr. Landers, what I would be like if I was allowed to become spoiled?"

His eyebrows shot up. "Yes. I think I can."

"Let me make sure. The army has really upset me. Some townspeople beat me up and almost killed me. The president disappointed me greatly. Congress has its moments that really get on my nerves. Some suppliers are not worth keeping alive, some of their workers included. I completely hate the taste of garbanzo beans and think the people who sell them as food should be prosecuted, at a minimum. Some people are bigoted against me simply because I have long hair and wear earrings, and I don't like anyone trashing my family." I gestured to show I was talking about the girls. "How would I handle those things if I didn't have these people to support me and teach me? How would a spoiled brat handle those things if he had the power to destroy anything and anybody he wanted, and no one would ever know? I'm personally glad that they're here, that they do a great job, and that they're zealous enough to be able to stop me if I go too far. It keeps me in check. So far, because of them, no one has been harmed, except maybe one army spy and fortunately, he didn't die."

"Putting it that way, I can see where they have their uses."

"One more thing," I said with a loving smile. "They love me, and they give great hugs."

He smiled. The rest of the girls were looking fondly at me. I had just stood up for them, and that meant a lot to each and every one.

The conversation changed to what was expected of everyone tomorrow. I started to volunteer for some things, but the captain said, "Freddy, you have the biggest job. Get that destroyer ready. I'm going to give you a choice. Which girl do you want to help you?"

I looked at her in puzzlement for a second and then said, "Excuse me?"

"I want one of the girls to help you with the mechanics and generally be with you. That will be her only duty. You want us to learn how to fix that ship in an emergency? Don't you think it would be good to have someone with you that you trained yourself?"

"Of course it would."

"Then choose."

Everyone looked at Marian, even the four who were reading the manuals. With a doctorate in aerospace engineering from Washington State and a doctorate in physics from Berkeley, she was the obvious first choice, but I could feel her emotions. She knew she was not the right one. Yes, she had degrees. But she was so far behind me that she couldn't keep up. We both discovered that while moving my home here. Her training from those two top institutions was the best but not in the right fields for this project. Besides, her degrees were useful in other requirements. I looked at her and said, "Marian, you're probably the most intelligent person here, but I need you to complete those scenarios and be the lead navigator on our destroyer. I'm sorry." I could feel her relief. This she could do well and would love it.

Marian said, "I understand. I'll get through those scenarios as quickly as possible, and I'll train the rest. Thank you, Freddy."

"Good, that's where you're needed the most … and you're welcome."

The admiral said, "Freddy, we were hoping to have you rename the destroyer to *Enterprise*."

"Not going to happen, Admiral. I'm saving that name for my first research-class aircraft carrier. Any other suggestions?"

I watched his eyebrows go up, and interest drifted across his face in what I would consider to be a "research class aircraft carrier," but he put that aside and said, "We also thought that the name *Protectress* would be good. 'Destroyer' sounds so bad to the public."

"What do you think, Marian? Would you like to be first navigator on the USS *Protectress*?"

"I'd like that, Freddy. I'd like that very much."

"Okay, then, the *Protectress* it is."

The admiral said, "Not 'USS,' Freddy. 'ES'—for Earth ship."

I looked over at Colleen and said, "Now, I wonder who came up with that idea?"

She blushed, and everyone laughed.

"Captain, there is a person here who has three degrees in engineering."

"Who?" the captain asked. "I know some of my team have three degrees each, and one has four, but none of the girls has three engineering degrees that I'm aware of."

I smiled and said, "She left it off her enlistment forms, Captain. I would bet she was hiding from having to be an officer because she really wanted to be a SEAL. I think we could change her mind if there was a position open, and we asked her to fill it. Chief engineer of the fleet and the ES *Protectress*—what a job that will be. We may start calling her Scotty. What do you think"—I turned my head slowly until I could look right into her eyes—"Chief Engineering Officer of the Fleet Patricia Henderson?"

She looked at me and started crying tears of happiness. She got up, came around the table, and picked me up.

I thought her hug was going to crush me. "Hey, you're breaking my bones, you know."

She loosened up but didn't let go. Finally, she held me out at arm's length and said, "Thank you. But the first person to call me Scotty will lose teeth."

The captain said, "Then it's settled, Chief Engineering Officer of the Fleet. Your job is to learn everything you can without slowing Freddy down."

"Yes, ma'am."

I added, "And to teach the others, because I expect all of you to come back with me and help me with the other ships and bases I'm building. I don't like changing personnel. Captain, after this project is completed, let's find a way to bring in some of the girls' families. I would feel better if they were closer. We can't expect them to never go home, never fall in love, or never have children of their own."

"We'll start planning for it. I'm sure Admiral Bates can find housing for us."

"Great! You know, this dish is wonderful." It was, but I was purposely changing the subject.

Cooky said, "You really like it, Freddy?"

"Yes. Can we have this one in the replicator?"

She smiled. "I'll get on it. I will also program some high-fat, high-carb meals."

I smiled. "Thanks."

"Not a problem. I expect to be the chief chef on the moon or Mars someday."

I smiled, "That's a good possibility. No matter how good the food is in the replicators, people will want freshly prepared meals. I could set you up with the first restaurant on the moon. Or better yet, you could be my personal chef and go wherever I go."

"Going where you go is a little too dangerous for me, but the first restaurant on the moon would be a fabulous idea."

"Well, you'll already be famous."

She looked at me and asked, "Why is that?"

"An entire fleet will be eating your recipes for years to come. The food programmed into the replicators will become one of two things."

Her eyes widened, and she said, "Famous or infamous, right?"

"Quite right, Cooky. Twenty-five recipes in only a few short hours—that's amazing."

"I think I'll work a little harder on the recipes."

"I'd suggest tasting the dishes yourself and then having others taste them. It's going to be a matter of eating each dish over and over and still enjoying it or having an extremely large menu so that no one gets bored with it. A big challenge, isn't it?"

"Yes, and I should be charging you extra."

"That's why I'm willing to put you into the first restaurant on the moon. You're doing us this favor. Whether you're successful or not is up to you. I doubt that people will want to flock to your restaurant if the food they eat on the way in the shuttles is second-rate or gives them intestinal problems, but we know that won't happen, will it?"

She looked at me in total fear for her career.

"You don't get a chance like this twice in life, Cooky. You're a great cook. You make the comfort food that people like to eat every day. You're going to do great. I'm just letting you know your options so that you can make informed choices. You're in the same situation that Henry and Dorothy are. I don't know if they will be going with us or not. That's up to the captain. I do know that the moon is going to need people with their qualities. So is the research ship that takes us to Mars and all the new planets."

The captain interjected, "Stick with us, ladies and gentlemen, and we'll make you famous."

Everyone laughed, but then Lieutenant Bergman said, "Or dead."

✦

Gray asked, "Is their food compatible with our metabolism."

I said, "*I hope so. We could use some changes.*"

Little Yellows giggled.

Green said, "Yes."

Gray smiled. "Great. Work on that replicator. My troops are bored with their rations."

Blue said, "The entire fleet is bored with the rations."

Yellows said, "Perhaps we should go back and capture this Cooky person."

Gray laughed. "Perhaps. Green, continue."

✦ ✦ ✦

CHAPTER 26

BEING HUMAN

I looked at Lieutenant Bergman with concern. "You seem to have some issues. If so, I want to know what they are."

"I'm sorry, Dr. Anderson. We've been talking about what you're doing. The job you've done is nothing short of fantastic, but we think you're going too fast. People aren't trained, nothing's been tested, this is all 'ifs'—*if* this works, and *if* we can do this, and *if* we get this. Right now, we've seen several faults in the thinking you have about space travel."

"Really? How interesting."

Denise said, "Oh no."

I looked at her and put my finger to my lips, cutting her off. "Lieutenant Bergman, I agree that I am going too fast, but I do not have a lot of choice, as the meteor is not slowing down. In your opinion, what do I have incorrect? If it could jeopardize the mission in any way, then we really need to know about it."

"I don't think I should say anything. It's not my place."

I raised my voice a little to get my point across as I addressed the entire group. "If anyone here has any ideas or thinks that something is not correct, then you have the right—in fact, is it your moral obligation—to speak up. If you do not speak, and it turns out that you were right, and people die because you did not have the guts to speak now, even though you may possibly be wrong, then you are jeopardizing this mission, the people involved in it, and possibly the entire human race. I want everyone's input, and I don't want you to hold back just because you're afraid of subjecting yourself to a little ridicule." I waited for their reaction, but everyone just stared at me in silence. Sighing heavily, I said, "Shop?"

"*Yes, Freddy?*"

"How many changes have I made due to input from the team or other sources?"

"*One thousand six hundred eighty-one.*"

"Thank you."

I looked at Lieutenant Bergman and lowered my voice. "I may be a child, but I'm not such a fool as to think that I know everything. Let's retire to the living room and listen to these issues that your group has, shall we?" I stood up, and so did everyone else. Dinner was about over anyway.

The captain said, "Cooky, we'll have dessert in the living room."

Cooky then looked at me and said, "That bread pudding I promised you." When I smacked my lips in anticipation, she laughed and whispered, "Listen to everything first, and think about your response. I don't want you to scare them away. They're doing us a lot of good."

I whispered back, "Gotcha." I looked at the lieutenant and asked, "Will it make things easier if you have a board to write on?"

"Yes, it would, thanks."

"Home?"

"*Yes, Freddy.*"

"Please open and energize the teaching board. Thank you."

On the wall a painting slid up so quickly that it startled the admiral and others. The team moved the small card table that was in front of the wall, and everyone sat down.

"I have several things to discuss," said Lieutenant Bergman. "First, we think your vision of what we will see when we travel faster than light is incorrect. All of our training indicates that it will be dark, not a blinding light, as your trainer suggests. If we go over the math, you can see ..."

He started to turn to the board, but I stopped him. "Lieutenant, do you mind if I show you something before you start working on your math? I think I can settle this issue fairly quickly."

"Please." He motioned for me to continue.

"Home?"

"Yes, Freddy?"

"Contact Shop and have her put onto this training board the view from the probes I sent off. Just one will do."

Instantly, several probes appeared on the screen, and then some disappeared. "Home, pause screen." The image stopped. "This is one of my probes. What you're seeing are the cameras and scanners documenting everything that the probe sees. Home, please remove the scanner views, and show the camera side and back views as separate blocks, interposed on the front view." The screens changed. "Note on the bottom screen that you can see the earth and twenty side views. Home, cut the side views to just four at ninety degrees from each other." The screen uncluttered, and now five views were interposed on the bottom of the front view. "Lieutenant, the probe saw the other probes disappear as they started traveling at faster than the speed of light. This one is just about to take off. Home, please resume."

The screen showed several other probes disappear, and then the screen went white, and the noise that was in the background increased tremendously. The back screen went as black as night, and the side screens showed nearly normal scenes. The probe shot past the moon. "Home, pause screen." I turned to Lieutenant Bergman. "You can see, from something that is actually traveling faster than the speed of light, that it is collecting all light, sound, and any other energy source as it moves forward. They bombard the front of the ship like it is moving through an ocean. In the rear view, it is totally dark, as light and other energies cannot catch up with the probe. The little flicker you catch every once in a while on the rear screen is an energy that is faster than the probe. I have not isolated that yet, but the army has all the information to do so. As you can see, the side views are fairly normal. In actuality, they are somewhat distorted, slightly stretched. The probes have the ability to analyze and adjust the input, but the light hits the sides almost at normal speed. The reason that the picture looks a little fuzzy is that the probe is traveling so fast that the friction from the light hitting the front of the probe's shields is affecting the side pictures. Any questions?"

"No, sir."

"Home, discontinue. Thank you."

"You're welcome, Freddy."

"Did that satisfy your confusion on that issue, Lieutenant?" I asked.

"Yes."

"Next issue, please."

The lieutenant was still staring at the blank screen. Captain James roused him by clearing her throat.

"Um, yes," the lieutenant said, "the next issue. We are having a hard time using your direction finder—the equipment that you use to plot a course. Sometimes it comes out wrong, and we have not been able to figure out why."

"Shop?"

"Yes, Freddy?"

"Please look back at the scenario in question."

"Working, Freddy."

A picture came up showing the plotting they were doing to make the trip to the nearest star. I watched with interest. They did nothing wrong. Someone said, "Engage." The ship started flying at mach seven. Shop said, *"Speeding up the view to the end."* They were nowhere near the system to which they plotted.

"Shop, did you investigate this?"

"Yes, Freddy. I found that the correct plot never gets us to the right place. I have checked the programming, and I could not see an issue."

"Place the math for long-distance plotting on the board and scroll at twenty-five."

Math showed up on the board and changed screens at twenty-five shots per minute. While I was watching, Lieutenant Bergman leaned over and asked Susan, "How can he see anything, let alone find a problem at this pace?"

She whispered back, "We don't know. We simply don't know."

"Stop!" I yelled. "Go back three screens." The image changed. "Whoops, I made a simple mistake. Shop, change the …" I started talking pure math to the computer. I talked the math, and the programming changed. It took about ten minutes. Meanwhile, the lieutenant sat down.

The captain said, "Shall we stop him?"

Dr. Landers said, "No, no, let him finish. This is fascinating. I have never in my entire life seen someone who could go through math like that. You do realize that he is having a conversation with the shop computer in pure physics. I doubt that any other person could do this at one-hundredth the speed. Also, he's using math techniques that are completely new. I can't understand much at this speed, and I'm considered one of the top mathematicians in the world. What I am getting is that some of the theorems we use are incorrect, and he has replaced them with laws that are correct."

Susan got up from her seat and picked up two books. She handed them to Dr. Landers, who looked at the covers and read out loud, *"Thoughts on Common Mistakes in Mathematical Beliefs* and *Math and Laws as God Set Them."* He thumbed through them. When he looked up, it was with eyes wide open, as if they were about to pop out. Several of the girls laughed. "How long have you had access to these?" he asked.

Marian said, "About two months now. I received them as a birthday present after I complained to Freddy that I could not figure out what I was doing wrong with some work he asked me to do. They're first editions. Actually, they're probably the only editions."

"Do you understand the importance of what's in these books?"

"Yes, I do, and Freddy made sure I understood every detail of what's in those books. Patricia and I both can nearly quote them from memory. I haven't had a problem with any project he's put me on since."

Colleen added, "When I saw *Math and Laws as God Set Them*, I asked him why that title. You know what he said? He said, 'Let's give credit to who wrote it. I was just the scribe.'"

Dr. Landers held the books to his chest. "Do you think he was kidding?"

"Freddy never jokes about work, and this was work. He said that God gave him the information to help with his projects. Looking at what he's accomplished, I can more easily believe that he accomplished all that with the help of God than I can believe that a child did it on his own."

Dr. Landers said, "That makes this holy scripture and

this project a holy mission." He looked at Freddy with renewed respect.

"Dr. Landers," said Marian, "you can read and copy anything you want from those books, but they are mine, and they don't leave this house. Freddy wrote them by hand— they're in his handwriting—and I believe that someday they will be worth more than I can ever know."

"Marian." Dr. Landers choked up and seemed at a loss for words. "Thank you."

"You're welcome, Doctor."

I said, "There. That should do it," They all looked at me. "Shop, run the programs again, and see what they do."

"*Running. Completed. That has corrected the problem. I will remove it from your to-do list.*"

"Thank you. I am so sorry, Lieutenant. I apologize to you and the team. I made a very critical error on page 205 that caused the math to be off all the way through page 912. I thought I'd tested that software, but I guess I only tested the short flight information that is installed on the first 150 pages. I am indebted to you, Lieutenant Bergman. Thank you."

He smiled. "Not a problem. Now … the third and last issue is somewhat of a more personal one. It's the reason that we're stuck on scenario fifty."

I smiled. "Go on."

"We all drop dead with no clue as to why. We have tried to figure out the reason, but I'm sorry to say we're stuck."

I looked puzzled. "That shouldn't happen. Let's go out to the trainer and find out why."

At the trainer, I said, "Let's man the systems just like you've been doing." They did, and I watched as they ran through the scenario. At one point the controls stopped working for them or slowed down a lot, and then they all died. I went over to the science officer and asked, "See this? What do you think it means?"

"Nitrogen level?" she asked. "I guess it means that the nitrogen level in the weapon systems is reaching critical."

"Why do you think it applies to the weapons?"

"This is the first scenario in which we've used the weapons this heavily, and it's the first time that indicator has moved up."

"Computer."

"*Yes?*"

"Help on the science console. What does the indication marked 'N$_2$' stand for?"

"*It indicates the level of nitrogen in the environmental pod.*"

"What would a high content of"—I looked at the indicator—"98 percent mean?"

"*That the environmental pods have a leak, and when they reach 94 percent, everyone on board will be dead very shortly if something is not done. At 98 percent, everyone should already be dead.*"

"What you experienced was a slowdown of controls, indicating that your reflexes were slowing down. At that point, some of the controls did not work because you were so groggy that you could not operate them correctly. You then died of asphyxiation. During an N$_2$ leak, you would have no idea it was your fault that everything was going nuts."

I walked over to the person in the captain's seat and said, "Your team member said 'I think.' Don't *think*! You had better *know*, or we're all dead. You're the captain, so you're fully responsible for the death of every member of this team."

She said, "We'll practice harder."

I put my hand on her shoulder and said, "Please finish this scenario tonight. I know you can do it. There's enough intelligence in this trainer right now that nothing should be impossible. Don't limit yourself. Make bold, unbelievable decisions! Make mistakes! Make all the mistakes you can, but learn from them. Personally, I can't believe you've figured out as much as you have, and because you have, I am nine weeks ahead of schedule on the *Protectress.*" That got a round of cheers. I could even hear them outside.

"Tomorrow I will sit in on scenario fifty-one and, hopefully, fifty-two also, and then I have work to do until you get to fifty-nine. I'm going to bed now. I need to rest. I expect to be up at 5:00 a.m. See you right after breakfast at 6:00 a.m. Patricia, you get some sleep too. It may be the last you get for a few days." I turned and walked out.

They followed me with their eyes. One said, "I love that kid."

I smiled.

✦

Yellows said, "*Math and Laws as God Set Them.*"

Little Yellows asked me mentally, "*Who and where is this God, young one?*"

"*He is everyone and everywhere.*"

Big Yellows continued. "We are back to the higher intelligence that is helping them. We need to know who, why, and where, and we need to know it now."

Little Yellows said, "This one does not know, and we doubt that any others do. He truly believes that this is his God and that it is everywhere."

Green said, "That means that finding this God is up to Gray."

Gray said, "We are on it."

Blue looked at Gray skeptically and said, "Continue, Green."

CHAPTER 27

✦ ✦ ✦

FTL

The next day I ran through scenarios fifty-one and fifty-two with them while showing them some things they hadn't considered. Then I said, "I need two crews, Captain—a three-person crew and a shuttle crew."

"What for, Freddy?"

"I was thinking last night that I can move ahead faster if I test out the FTL drives before I go any further on the *Protectress*. Therefore, I want to take up one of the Sting Rays and follow it with a shuttle. We will be going faster than light this time. No human has ever done this before, so this is going to be a record, and the danger involved is very high."

The captain said, "It's almost lunchtime. Will right after lunch be okay?"

"Yes. Do you think you can get volunteers for this?"

"Freddy, every person on this team and the NASA volunteers have come to me at one time or another this week, begging to be the first to fly at speeds faster than light. Well, everyone except you."

I looked at her with wide eyes and then smiled. I turned around, heading for the house and lunch, mumbling, "Nut cases. Suicidal maniacs. I'm being protected and assisted by crazies."

The mood was high as we ate. After lunch I went with Patricia into the workshop, and we flew out a Sting Ray. As we came out of the ship, I said to the captain, "This is the plan."

She stopped me, saying, "Scenario number eight."

"Exactly," I said.

"The teams are standing by."

"Then let's go."

Both teams went to their ships. I noted with pride that all three on the Sting Ray team were my girls. The three astronauts were with the shuttle. I took a seat in the back and watched. Patricia was with me, and I started teaching her things about the shuttle design and the way I had built it.

The captain said, "Freddy?"

I looked up from a panel that I had removed. "Yes?"

"We're ready. You're not messing with the ship, are you?"

I put the panel back on and said, "Not while we're underway, Captain."

We were eight hundred miles up and climbing fast. The Sting Ray that they named *Manta* was already at one thousand miles up and holding. The captain started giving orders. "Give me communications to *Manta*."

"This is *Manta*. Hear you loud and clear. Everything is normal and ready to go."

The captain said, "We're coming up behind you now. Plot for Mars, and take off at one hundred miles per hour."

"Plotted. Engaging."

In the front screen, I saw them move away slowly.

I said, "Captain, scans show they're at a hundred miles per hour."

"How's that feel, *Manta*?" asked the captain.

"No feeling at all, Captain."

"Navigator, follow her at a hundred miles per hour, and continue to follow one step behind her speed. Engage. *Manta*, kick her up to one thousand miles per hour."

"Engaged."

I reported, "Scans show she's at one thousand miles per hour."

The captain ordered, "Report, *Manta*."

"We're at one thousand miles per hour, and we've had no adverse feelings. The ship is running true, and everything is normal. Man, I wish I had a car that could instantaneously accelerate like this."

"Kick her up to half impulse, *Manta*."

"Engaged."

I reported, "Captain, she's moving away at fifty million miles per hour."

"*America's Dream*, we're reporting that the ship is still running true, with all controls and indicators at normal."

"Good. Kick her up to full impulse, *Manta*."

"Engaged."

I was impressed that there were no extreme emotions, particularly fear, from the crew.

"Captain, this is *Manta*. We are at full impulse, and the scanners show that we're traveling at just over 160 million miles per hour."

"Our scanners confirm, Captain."

"Catch up then, Navigator."

"Going to full impulse, Captain."

I could just barely feel that we were moving faster.

I reported, "Scanners show that our full impulse is 210 million miles per hour, Captain. I am logging it in."

"This is *Manta*. My scanners confirm 210 million. I have slowed down so that you can catch me more quickly. I will speed up to full impulse when you are within two clicks."

Navigations said, "Captain, we are coming up on *Manta*

and expect to synchronize in four, three, two, one … we are now synchronized at 150 million miles per hour."

"*Manta*, report," said the captain.

"This is *Manta*. All is go; I repeat, all is go. Indicators show normal with no vibrations. Environmental is normal, and navigation shields are on high. Have plot for high orbit around Mars. Plot is confirmed."

"Good luck, team. Engage at warp one."

They disappeared from the normal screens, but the science officer quickly changed to scanners, and they showed up fine.

"This is *Manta*. Everything is normal, but we felt a little movement at first, just a tiny bit, and our screens went blank while turning over to scanners."

I said, "I can adjust that out, and I will do that for the screens, but I thought you would want some feeling when you change directions or speed. I remember several times that you guys said that you like driving the jeeps instead of the limousines because you can feel the road with the jeeps."

"That's good, Freddy. Just get the screens right. It made things a little freaky for a second or two."

"Sorry."

The captain said, "*Manta*, increase to warp two."

"Engaged."

"Navigator, engage." The shuttle hit light speed instantly. It was kind of anticlimactic.

"Twenty miles above high orbit at Mars in ten minutes, Captain."

"*Manta* is at warp two."

"Navigator, increase to warp two."

We felt just the tiniest movement, but it was very irritating and made my head hurt. I jumped down, and Patricia followed me.

The captain said, "That didn't feel good, Freddy."

"I know, Captain. We're on it. The adjustment is all wrong." I was mumbling to myself and then said, "Captain, please have *Manta* not make orbit. Continue straight for a few minutes until we catch up to her."

"Did you get that *Manta*?"

"We got it. Holding steady at warp two."

I said, "Captain, go to warp one, please." I opened a panel. "Patricia, these are the dampeners." She whistled low with appreciation. "If you look at these monitors, you will note that I have the adjustments set at just short of zero. There are forty adjustments, covering all directions. I have several set too high. Let's adjust them down to about .02 percent of G1."

"Okay, Freddy."

I stepped back. "Go ahead, Patricia, but be very careful because adjusting it wrong could be very bad."

She looked at me with a smile and reached in. She adjusted each to exactly .02, and it only took a couple of seconds each. I couldn't have adjusted them that quickly. She was very good.

"Captain, please increase to warp two."

"Navigator, engage."

I felt just a tiny bit of movement but not enough to cause any pain this time.

"How's that, Captain?" asked Patricia.

"A little lower please. Navigator, drop to warp one."

I felt a slight slowing movement.

Patricia adjusted everything down to .015. "Try that, Captain."

"Navigator, warp two, please."

It was just barely noticeable, but I could feel that there was a change in speed.

"That's good, Patricia," said the captain.

I showed Patricia how to lock things down, and we closed the panel and returned to our seats.

The captain turned around and looked at me. "Freddy, can we increase to warp five safely?"

"Sure, Captain. If warp two worked, then all the others should be fine."

"*Manta*?"

"Yes, Captain?"

"Let's play tag. Power up weapons, and set them at warning, with shields on high. All speeds authorized. Go." The reports then went just to *America's Dream. Manta* went silent.

"*Manta* has increased her speed to warp seven."

"Catch her, Navigator. Weapons Officer, stand by to give her a warning shot as soon as she comes into range. Shields at max."

"Increasing speed to warp 8.5."

"Shields up, Captain."

"Weapons on line, set for a warning shot, Captain."

"She's heading for some asteroids."

"Bold move. How long before we're in range, Weapons Officer?"

"Three minutes, Captain."

"How long before she reaches the asteroid field?"

"One minute and eight seconds."

"Captain, I have something else on screen coming in fast."

"Break off pursuit, and go on the offensive. Science Officer, I want to know what's out there."

"Working on it."

"Captain, this is the *Manta*. Are you in trouble?"

"*Manta*, we're not alone."

"I see her, Captain. What do you want to do?"

"You're wingman, *Manta*. Take up position."

"On my way, Captain."

"Captain, the ship is one of the types that have been seen

dropping off supplies to the mother ship at home. Shall I put her on screen?"

"Do it." The screen showed a craft, bulky and slow, coming in from the third quadrant.

"Science, is she chasing us?"

"Checking. She has a trajectory that suggests a high orbit around Earth. I don't think she's seen us, Captain."

"We can't just sit out here until she unloads and goes away. Freddy does not have the time, and neither do we. *Manta*, take up position on her right and back far enough to let her know you're following but not hostile. We're going home with Freddy."

"Will do, Captain." *Manta* quickly changed course and within minutes slid right behind the other ship and slightly off to her right.

"Navigator, I want to run right by her at warp seven. Bring us home, but let her know that *Manta* is not the only ship out here that can catch her."

On the screen I could see us shoot past the other ship, and she changed course just a little but went right back on track.

"I hope I made her nervous enough that she'll think twice about firing on *Manta*. Warn the base we're coming in and have three more *Manta*-class ships prepped and ready to go. I don't want my girls up here alone."

Before we reached home, Science reported that three more Stingers were headed our way and would take up positions around the cargo vessel within two minutes.

"Freddy, you really did a nice job building these ships."

"Thanks, Captain, but I'm still afraid that one will be set wrong and possibly harm people."

"Good. Keep worrying. That's what made these ships work the first time. Do you realize how many records we broke today?"

"Nope. Several, I suspect."

She shook her head and whispered to the navigator, "He really doesn't care that his ships just made history."

✦

Gray asked, "Who is this other species they are talking about? Could it be their God?"

I laughed.

Little Yellows said, "It's not their God. That we can assure you."

Gray asked, "Are you getting information from the creature?"

Big Yellows asked, "Where have you been for the last two hours, Gray? Our pen mate is constantly watching the creature."

Little Yellows said, "He thinks you're funny, Gray."

Gray started fuming. Blue said, "Yellows, if Gray becomes upset, kill him. We will obtain another."

Gray quickly calmed down. "I am not upset. This creature seems to have a strange sense of humor."

Yellows said, "Actually, we find you funny sometimes also. Green, continue."

Green said, "This is the first time they ever flew faster than light. We have statues of our Red and worship his remembrance. It is remarkable that they developed ships that exceed our own so quickly."

Blue said, "Perhaps they simply went down a different direction in their thinking and hit on something better, or it may be this God creature. Whichever it is, we will not find out unless you continue."

CHAPTER 28

✦ ✦ ✦

A VISIT FROM FRIENDS

Patricia and I discussed the equipment and what had to be done to keep the ships up and running. We opened several panels, and I pointed out many items. Before we knew it, the captain was telling us that we had landed and could disembark.

I said, "Already? Oh well, time to go to work."

The captain stopped me to ask, "Freddy, can we have one of the bigger ships to start a patrol?"

"Susan, you can have anything you want. Just be careful out there." I started to turn away but stopped and said. "One more thing … I want to be the first to set foot on another planet. Mars will do fine, but I want to be the one."

She smiled and said, "I think you have earned that right. I'll make it clear to everyone. You have guests, Freddy. It's not work time yet."

"Guests? Who?"

"Captain Crain and his family. They came in on his boat. He needed some repairs and hoped you could help install a new engine using your lifts. Otherwise, he'd have needed to wait for the floating crane, and that would have taken at least a month."

"Are we helping him?"

"We're almost finished. He should be ready to leave in just a few hours. They're going to have dinner with us in about half an hour."

"Cool! I'll have time to play with Annabelle and Johnny. Let's go."

"Becky's here too," Susan pointed out.

"And so, I assume, are Mrs. Crain and Carroll. What's your point, Captain?"

"Ouch! I can feel the tension, Freddy. If you want, I can say you're too locked up in an experiment to see them now."

"No, Captain. But thank you. My mommy taught me once that running away from things only puts them off until they catch you, and she said, 'They always catch you.' I would prefer catching them first, here on my own turf, in my own way. I won't pretend that I don't have feelings for Becky because I do, but I won't allow my feelings to get in the way of good friendships. You taught me that once, remember?"

"Yes, I do. Very well. Are you ready to see them?"

"As ready as I can possibly be."

"Then here we go."

We left the ship, and Patricia held my hand. Outside, she lifted our joined hands to cheers and applause. The whole team was there, minus the ones on watch and in the ships. They were cheering me about my success on being the first to build a ship that traveled faster than light. I received many pats on the back and a ride on the lieutenant's shoulder all the way to the house.

When we reached the house, she put me down in front of Mrs. Crain. I could feel that Mrs. Crain felt totally out of her league. "Congratulations, Freddy! We watched on your scanners," Mrs. Crain said. "What you've done is remarkable! Actually, it's so totally unbelievable, I don't know what to say."

"Congratulations will do nicely," I said, and I gave her a great big hug. That broke the ice, and everyone started talking at once.

Johnny asked, "Did you really fly in space?"

"Farther and faster than anyone ever flew before. Fun, isn't it?"

"Really fun," he replied.

I reached down and said hello to Annabelle, and she returned my greeting with a big hug and a "hi." I waved to the others and said, "Hi, Carroll! Hi, Becky! It's nice to see you again. Welcome to my home, everyone." Before they could say anything, I took Annabelle's hand and started into the house. "My, but you've grown. How long has it been?"

I looked back at the captain, and she whispered, "Eight months."

"Eight months," I said. "No wonder you're taller. Soon, I'll be looking up to you!" She had the biggest smile. We stepped inside and went to the living room and talked for several minutes. Johnny and Carroll asked questions, and so did Mrs. Crain, and I answered as many as I could without giving away the world's plight.

When dinner was ready, Captain Crain and the team came in. He said, "I can't believe how easy that was. We should be ready to go as soon as dinner is over. Hello, Freddy."

"Hi, Captain Crain. How's fishing these days?"

I quickly learned that's a good question to ask him, as he monopolized most of the dinner conversation, talking about the tides, water temperatures, depths where the fish are, and everything else you could imagine. Plus some things you couldn't—like catching a great white in the nets with the salmon. He was just finishing up that story when Mrs. Crain interrupted him to point out that he hadn't even touched his dinner. "Yes, dear," he responded.

I was disappointed when he stopped talking and started eating.

Becky drew attention to herself by asking for the butter. It was right in front of me, so I picked it up and passed it to her. When she thanked me, I responded pleasantly, "My pleasure." Ensuring that I kept my voice the same as I used with everyone else, I asked her, "How's school going, Becky?"

She suddenly started to cry, got up from the table, and ran from the room. A team member left to watch her. I looked at Captain James, and she said, "It's nothing you did, Freddy. It's a girl thing."

Annabelle added, "Becky's in love with another boy, and she didn't want to come here because she's afraid that Freddy is mad at her."

"I know, Annabelle." I said, "She loves Jimmy."

Johnny said, "No, silly. That was ages ago."

Carroll added, "Four boyfriends ago. It's David now."

Colleen asked, "Freddy, what's going through your mind right now?"

I looked up at her and said, "First, I was thinking that it wasn't my always being gone that caused Becky to break up with me, was it?"

"No, I guess not," Colleen agreed.

"That means that someday I'll have a chance for love that will last." I nearly had a tear in my eye.

Colleen hugged me and said, "Of course you will."

"Then I was thinking, there's something wrong if Becky is going through boyfriends that quickly. What is it?" I stood up and went outside. Marian was out there and pointed to where Becky was. I went over and sat down next to her. I put my arm around her and probed her mind. It was easy to see the problems once I knew what to look for. I hugged her and said, "Becky, you're wrong you know. Your daddy does love you. I can feel it, and you feel it also, don't you?"

"Yes."

"He loves you more than you'll ever know. Not more or less than the other three kids but just as much. When he leaves, you're last on his mind; you're right there. However, it's not because he loves you less; it's because he trusts you more. He knows how intelligent and sweet you are, and he knows he can trust you to do what's right. I felt it in him when he left before. I wish I could generate that kind of trust. Here, I am stuck with fifty babysitters, and the numbers are growing every day. He can leave you alone because he believes in you. You're very lucky. Stop trying to hurt men just because your daddy hurts you when he leaves. You're a heartbreaker, and take it from me: it hurts."

"I'm sorry," she said.

"Don't ever try to lie to me, Becky. You're not sorry. You wanted to hurt me to get attention. Did it work?"

"Yes. For a little while."

"Was that little while worth it, or are you hurting yourself more?"

"It was good at the beginning, but then it just went back to the way it was before. Only now I've lost a good friend."

"Really? Who?"

"You, silly."

"You haven't lost me as a friend. Just as a boyfriend for now. I hope we can always be good friends, Becky."

She turned to me and gave me a hug. We sat there a while, holding each other. Before the Crain family left, I told Captain Crain and Mrs. Crain what I'd found out. It was up to them now.

As soon as they left, Susan took me inside and sat down with me. "What's wrong with Becky?"

I told her what I'd found out and what I'd done. I let her know I was worried about Becky and what she was doing to herself. "She's empathic, Susan, and it's affecting her. Every boy that likes her, she likes. It's going to be hard on her."

Susan hugged me, and so did almost everyone else. Afterward, I asked Susan if there were any more people I could help who would give me hugs like that. They all laughed.

I said, "Time to go to work." I headed out to the workshop. Patricia was right behind me.

✦

Green said, "The creature is very affectionate."

Little Yellows said, "You have no idea." To me, they said, "Stop trying to get free, or we will stop letting you see and hear."

Gray asked, "What is a 'floating crane'?"

Blue's eyes circled as if going completely around inside his head—to the right and back from the left. The long look on his face and the eyes nearly screamed annoyance.

Green smiled while looking away from Gray, and it said, "Floating would be something that sits on the top of the water, and a crane would be something that can lift heavy objects. I would bet that a floating crane is something to lift the possibly heavy motor out of the boat and put a new one in."

Green nearly burst out with laughter when Gray said, "Makes sense."

I said to little Yellows, "*Finally, Green got one correct.*"

Little Yellows nearly dropped me in their amusement.

Big Yellows asked, "What is so funny, my friend?"

Little Yellows said, "Green is correct."

"What is so funny about that?"

"For the first time."

They all laughed except Green, who looked displeased and continued with the probing.

CHAPTER 29

FIRST ENCOUNTER FACE-TO-FACE

We came out two days later when the captain summoned us. She met us at the door and said, "Freddy, you need to see this." We went inside to the living room. "Play that tape back."

At first, it was just a scanner tape of the base, but as we watched, the tape showed a push in the side of the shield—not big but a definite bump. Something had tried to get in but could not. Something we could not see. It tried several times. I became excited and said, "Shop?"

"Yes, Freddy?"

"Bring the main scanners online at full power."

"Working. Scanners online."

"Good. Now show me."

"Working. Patching through the house monitor." We all turned that way. Nothing showed.

"Shop, toggle through the entire spectrum. Pinpoint and show anything that cannot be seen in this mode."

"Working. Found two objects."

On the screen was a ship of unknown origin and

a creature that looked like nothing I'd ever seen. It was under the water with its ship and testing my shield. "Very interesting. Shop, place a shield around it and a separate shield around its ship. Can we sense that creature?"

"*Compliance. Yes, under eighteen different modes.*"

The creature turned quickly and tried to escape but could not.

"Shop, bring it and its ship to the surface. Leave its ship at the open platform on the other side of the helipads, but keep it shielded. Bring the creature to me."

"*Compliance.*"

"Shop, scan the ship. Are there any more living beings in it?"

"*No, Freddy.*"

"Freddy, are you sure this is a good idea?" Susan asked.

"Yes. It cannot get out of the shield, and we can easily kill it, if necessary. Just order Shop to decrease the size of the shield's inner diameter to one foot, but don't let it loose until I check it out."

I turned to Katie, who immediately said, "I'm with you, Freddy."

"Monitor my mind," I told her, "and if I start acting weird, knock me out."

"Will do."

"Shop," said Susan, "if Katie knocks Freddy out, then instantly destroy that creature."

"*Understood.*"

We went outside and watched as the creature was slowly brought to us. It looked frightened.

When I reached the creature, it had folded up on itself a little. I touched its mind; the thoughts were very different from ours, but the basics were there. It was afraid—that was easy to see. "Shop?"

"*Yes, Freddy?*"

"Allow two-way communications, please."

"*Completed.*"

I looked at the creature. It was unique and kind of pretty in a different sort of way. It had wings that radiated different colors, like a translucent butterfly. The torso was almost manlike, but I could easily tell it was a water creature by the fins and long, flat webbed feet and hands. I could see the strength in the limbs, but at the same time, it looked delicate. I said, "Hello."

It turned toward me and said, "Hello, Freddy Anderson. My name is Bubble Maker."

"You know me, and you speak English? You are one of our friends who lives under the sea?"

"Yes, friends. You were on television several times."

"Why are you trying to break into my home?"

"Your shields are better than anything we have ever encountered. We are interested. My captain asked me to look into it. I am doing so."

"You are at war with another?"

"Yes. How did you know?"

"My scanners picked something up that made me believe so. How is the war going?"

"Badly for our side. We have lost many ships."

"Why are you here on this planet?"

"We are assigned to protect your world."

"But you are leaving. Why?"

"We cannot stop the asteroid that is headed your way, and the war is going badly so we are needed back at home. I am sorry, Freddy Anderson."

"The asteroid is nothing, so don't worry. I can destroy it. You want the shield technology before you pull out and it's lost forever. Is this correct, my friend?"

"Yes. Can you really destroy the asteroid?"

"You have seen some of my new ships. Did you think we would sit around and do nothing?"

I don't know if I would call the creature's expression a smile, but it felt that way mentally. "My captain said that this race would never give up."

"You speak very good English."

"I have been stationed here for forty-three of your years."

"I will be right back." I smiled and said, "Don't go away."

I went into the workshop, with Susan and Patricia right behind me again.

"What are you planning to do?" asked Susan.

"I'm going to give Bubble Maker a goodwill present. I'm giving him the technology to the shield around my home."

"Freddy, I don't like that idea."

"Don't worry, Susan." I ran back out before she could stop me. "Shop, allow this to go through the shield." I levitated the disk and moved it toward the shield. It passed right through and into his hand. He placed it in a pouch. I told him, "That is the complete technology and directions for building the shield."

He looked at me and said, "Thank you, Freddy Anderson, our friend."

"Call it a goodwill present. Please come back and see us some time."

"We will. We are very interested in your race as friends. We have much to learn from one another. At the beginning of this war, we were lost, as we do not fight between ourselves. It is your bad example that has saved us. We studied your tactics." He patted his pouch, "This will give us the advantage. Something we have never had before."

I raised my hand and said, "Shields up, Bubble Maker."

"Good luck, Freddy Anderson."

"Shop, please take this one and his ship back to where we captured him, and let him go." I waved good-bye as he drifted back into the sea, and then I ran back into the house and watched as he entered his ship and left.

✦

Gray said, "That was unexpected. The creature seems very giving. Perhaps we could ask it the questions instead of probing. It would be much quicker."

I said nothing and tried to shield my mind.

Little Yellows said, "That might have worked if we'd come to his planet as friends instead of attacking immediately. We are now the enemy, and he has an obligation to not tell us. Note how we find out about his life but not details on technology."

Green said, "This is correct. So far, he has given up less than any other."

Gray said, "I must agree with Yellows. We should have befriended them first or at least tried." All stared at the Gray. "What? You don't think we recognize a good tactic when we see one?"

Almost everyone in the room said, "*No!*"

Yellows said, "Green, continue."

✦ ✦ ✦

NEW EQUIPMENT

Susan stood nearly directly over me, like an angry, muscle-bound pit bull towering over a newborn kitten. She was just about to read me the riot act for giving him the ability to get through our shields, so I looked at her and, in a shaky voice, said, "Shop?"

"*Yes, Freddy?*"

"Scan the entire area for any potential hazards if we were to drop our shields."

"*Scanned. There are no issues at this time. The creature has left.*"

"Good. Please drop the temporary shields, and start up the main shields."

From the watch room, I could hear a whistle, so we all went that way. Denise was on watch, and as we entered, she said, "Captain, I don't know what happened, but I was watching the screens, and they just went out. Within a second, they came up on a new mode. Look! We still have the main screen, but now we have five others showing other styles of scanning, and the shield changed. The scanners show that it's over a thousand times stronger and totally different."

"Keep up the good work, and learn these screens so you can train your watch relief."

"Yes, ma'am."

I went into the kitchen. After two days without eating, I was hungry. Patricia was already there, eating. Susan followed me, and so did the admiral. Susan asked, "Freddy, when were you going to tell me about the new shields and scanning system?"

"I don't know," I said. "I had forgotten about them. No one can sneak up on us again, Captain. Not with these shields and scanners. These are the new version that I put in the destroyer. Oh, by the way, I need to bring it out soon. You wouldn't happen to have fifty people you can loan me for a couple of days, would you?"

Patricia's entire face lit up with her smile. She knew I was trying to change the subject, and she knew the captain would never go for it.

Susan said, "Listen to me, Freddy. You ever do that again, and I'll personally turn you over to the lieutenant for a good over-the-knee session. Now, why did you do that?"

"First, I'm sorry a little but not much. Second, the oxygen in the water was depleting quickly, and the creature was going to suffocate soon if I didn't hurry. Third, he was afraid of what we'd do to him. They have been caught before, and it's never a good thing. Fourth, the present I gave him will help him hold his own against the others in their war. Fifth, the others are the ones who shot down my probe. Sixth, I needed a distraction, and that meant working fast, before he could think about it and start checking. You see, my computer had negotiated with his onboard computer and downloaded everything in the mother ship's computers.

As soon as I found out he was in constant communication with the main vessel, I contacted Shop mentally and put in the request. For that little gift we gave so freely and kindly, we received information about them and their allies and enemies, all of their technology, and, if I'm not mistaken, images of our history for the last three thousand years. I did not have time to ask permission, and he is slightly telepathic, only open thoughts. Still, discussing it in committee would have ruined the chance. Now the question is this: are we going to give this away to the army too?"

The admiral said, "I certainly hope not!"

Susan said, "Freddy, you did a good thing this time, but you must be very careful. We can't just give away our technology."

"I know, but it's the only thing I could think of, and besides, I invented that shield and scanner on the spur of the moment when I was upset with the army. They are nothing compared to the ones I developed, once I had a few hours to sit down and think the problem through. All I gave away was a toy shield, compared to what we now have."

Cooky brought me some pasta, and I started eating. Bed was going to feel good tonight. The admiral motioned for the captain to follow him out. Susan said, "We'll talk later, Freddy."

"Okay, boss," I responded. "I'm not going anywhere."

When the admiral had the captain in the other room, he said, "Susan, he invented the shields as a spur-of-the-moment thought?"

"Yes, Admiral, and the shield around us now is probably nuke–proof."

The lieutenant walked in and said, "Yes, it is." They both looked at her. "I was just in training, and that shield has a warning system that it activates in case of nuclear attack. Captain, the shield is 360 degrees. We're in a bubble right now."

"How deep does it extend?"

"It's not a perfect sphere, Captain. It's only about five thousand feet deep, and it covers the entire top, partly out to sea, and some of the surrounding forest. It's not setting anything on fire, as it's not energy, as far as we can tell. It's like a plastic bubble that can be controlled. It's multidirectional. In short, we can go in or out or both, depending to how we set it at any grid. We can modulate it to make it visible or we can make it invisible, even to the scanners but not to his new scanners. They are something else."

"What do you mean?" asked Susan.

"The range has been increased. They reach out over eighty light-years instantly and can detect moving objects up to 130 light-years away, and at the same time it's detecting something at a distance, it can tell you everything around you too. Right down to the smallest atom. If the other scanners were spur-of-the-moment, then he put a lot of thought into the new ones."

"And these are on the new ships?" asked the admiral.

"He said they were, so expect it."

I had finished eating, so I came into the living room on my way up to bed. "Think twice about who controls the *Protectress*, Captain. That person will be the second most powerful person in the known universe. I would hate to have to destroy him or her."

As I went up to bed, three people watched me, with chins dropped to their ankles.

✦

Gray motioned for another Gray to come over and then said, "Go check to see if our computers are transmitting to their ships. *Now!*"

I smiled.

Little Yellows said, "we would bet they are."

Green yelled, "Shut down all computer transmitting capabilities immediately! If they have our information, we are in deep trouble."

A voice came over the intercom. "Gray One. It is too late. The ship they had following us left minutes ago. The transmissions stopped at about the same time. They have everything."

"Follow that ship, and destroy it. Turn the fleet around. *Do it!*"

Black slid in and said in a very quiet voice, "Do not follow that ship. It is his fastest, and they are already sending the information to their fleet and home world. It is also transmitting to seventeen other worlds."

Gray ordered, "Do not follow the ship. Head for home at all possible speed. We are doomed."

Little Yellows said, "We don't think so. Let us continue. We believe we will find a way around this."

Black ordered as he slid out, "Then continue."

CHAPTER 31

✦ ✦ ✦

BIG ISSUE, BIG DEAL!

The next two months were spent mostly in the workshop. Patricia was coming along fine. The *Protectress* was ready to come out right after we snatched some rest. Patricia and I came out about two in the afternoon, when Shop gave us a warning.

"The captain asked me to relay this information to you as soon as you were available but not until you were finished with this juncture of work. Freddy, while you were working on the Protectress, *the media found out about the rock, and they nicknamed it 'the Destroyer.'"*

"Well, figure the odds on that."

"I have, and it's 123,345,187.93 to one."

"Very well. Continue."

"The president had a press conference to calm down the public. She told them that a private organization is working on the situation."

"Nice. Since I'm the only private organization that has the technology, they automatically aimed in my direction."

"That's about it."

"Is the base under attack?"

"No. The captain has made it very clear that they stay away. She has told them that you will talk to them as soon as possible."

"I'm going to have to placate them somewhat. Shop, please contact my lawyers."

"Working."

A nice alto voice said, "Zimmer and Venski Law Offices. How may I help you?"

"Hello, this is Freddy Anderson. Is Jeff or Carl there?"

"They've been expecting your call. I'll put you right through."

"Freddy, nice to hear from you. Seems we have a small problem. My offices are under attack. I have lawyers suing us for information. We have people outside holding picket signs with sayings like 'Let Freddy Talk to Us' and 'Help Us, Freddy.'"

"Working for me is interesting, isn't it?"

"Yes, it is. Want a report?"

"Sure."

"You made $119 million off that lawsuit against the media and put 40 percent of them in the red. Most paid, but several filed bankruptcy. The media has formed a new group called Honesty and Fairness in the News, and get this—they have asked the public to pick people to run the group. It's based on the medical system. You now need to pass an exam and take a moral oath to 'report completely and fairly' before you receive a license to report the news, to own a news group, or to edit the news. If you do something majorly wrong, you go before a board of your peers, and they can yank your license."

"That's nice, but who can we trust to cover us in this crisis?"

"That's easy. Five of the 'Big Ten' paid quickly, with

promises of their full and complete cooperation if they can get coverage of any breaking news."

"Send me a fax on them, and include phone numbers to call. I need to talk to my people, but very soon I will need coverage on the greatest breakthrough in history. Has the army complied with giving news only to these five?"

"Yes. They've been very adamant about that. They hold exclusives, claiming that you insisted. They don't invite the ones that are not cooperating, and they don't let them into the meetings. Still, the others obtain the information through lawsuits and off the other groups' news sites. The army complied with the freedom-of-the-press lawsuits about two days after the news was first given out. Therefore, they got the information days later than the others, and that is killing them."

"Good job, guys."

"Freddy, we have a favor to ask."

"Go ahead."

"We have other problems besides what you're working on. The world thinks that you're gay."

"What?"

"They keep seeing you in long hair and wearing earrings and have asked hundreds of questions about it. You were wearing dangly earrings during the 'Ghost Hunt.' We receive mail every day condemning you for it and some praising you, but we receive the most mail saying that you're gay and strongly suggesting you 'get a haircut and stop acting like a girl, or else.'"

"Interesting. I bet it's going to rankle some people that the 'child' who is going to save them is someone who doesn't quite match their expectations."

"Yes, it will, and it will draw attention to you in other ways. Especially since they think you are gay."

"Why? I've never even had sex. How can they make that judgment?"

"It's stupid, we know. But they draw their conclusion from the fact that you look rather feminine. Face it. You look like a very lovely young girl with your hair long and wearing earrings."

"Close-minded bigots! So using that argument, are all women who have short hair and don't wear earrings gay?"

"No. It only applies to men."

"Really. Why not both ways?"

"The men are used to women doing what they want, so it must be okay."

"I can't believe it! Here I am, attempting to save the world, and this is the big issue."

"Not the big issue, but it ranks up there."

"What do you guys suggest?"

"Either get your hair cut and stop wearing earrings, or make a big deal out of this in some fashion. Take the question and the mystery out of it, and the issue will calm down."

"I'll talk to my leaders about it."

"Thanks."

"Bye, guys."

"Bye, Freddy. Let us know when you're going to hold a press conference. We need to be there."

"You got it. Bye."

"Thank you, Shop."

"*You're welcome, Freddy.*"

I turned to Patricia and said, "Interesting conversation."

"Yes, wasn't it?" she replied. "What do you plan to do about it?"

"Talk to the boss, and see what she thinks. I have to have my hair long, as the energy that builds up in the protein increases my ability to heal and use telekinesis. My mother and father wore earrings and had long hair. It's hard enough to speak in front of all those people, let alone try to explain why I do what I do or am what I am."

We went out and were immediately met by the captain and admiral. I was just a little depressed about the situation, and receiving threatening mail is horrible.

Susan said, "You weren't gone long, Freddy. Only four days."

I think she was about to chew me out for working so long without a rest again, so I said, "We're finished, Susan."

"Finished?"

I reached over and shook hands with the admiral. "Hello, Admiral, sir."

"Hello, Freddy, nice to see you."

I turned to Susan and said, "The ship is ready for loading and for her maiden voyage. I will bring her out after we get something to eat, some sleep, and fix a problem or two. Right now, we seem to have a media issue. Am I right?"

"Yes. The president wants to talk to you as soon as possible."

"Might as well talk while I'm eating. She'll understand. Patricia has been the best helper, Captain. I couldn't have finished without her. Not this quickly." I took a deep breath and then said, "Shop?"

"*Yes, Freddy?*"

"Play back that conversation we just had with Zimmer and Venski for the captain, please."

They listened, and Susan whistled. "That figures. I kind of expected it would come up eventually."

I said, "It's silly. Now that we're finished, I suppose we need to have a press conference."

"Whenever you're ready." She could see my mind wasn't on the project.

"I guess the day after tomorrow will be good. I don't

want it set up here, but I want to be ready to have the media come to the base right after."

"Why?"

"How much hate mail have I received here at home, Susan?"

She blushed, and I knew it was quite a lot. I told her what I planned to do, and she nearly died. The admiral was in shock, but Patricia just smiled and said, "You think that's bad. Try having a twenty-foot robotic spider jump out at you!"

Susan sobered up quickly and looked at me with a frown. Man, she can change moods quickly. I took off running. I remembered what she said she'd do if I didn't stop playing my jokes. It was no good, though. I could not outrun her, and I sat at the table with a sore bottom as the video call went through for the president.

When the call was connected, I said, sounding disheartened, "I hear you want to talk to me. Madam President."

"Yes, Freddy. First, I want to apologize for giving away who was working on getting us out of this fix."

"As I understand it, you said nothing wrong, Madam President. The media took that, along with our discoveries that the army has published and our breakthrough with traveling faster than light, and put two and two together— and they actually got four this time."

She smiled and said, "Something like that."

"I would have loved to have been there when the admiral took the media for a flight around Mars. That must have been fun. I hear we have some issues."

"Yes. I can't keep this quiet any longer. We need to give them something to calm the public down. They know about your small ships, but they also believe that they can't stop this 'Destroyer.' It's becoming a public nightmare."

"Madam President, please let them know that I am going to hold a press conference the day after tomorrow. The captain is setting it up." I told the president what I planned to do, and she just about had a hissy fit.

"Freddy, that would not be a good thing."

"Well, you'll be there to help calm me down, won't you?"

"Yes."

"You're losing in the polls, aren't you?"

"Yes. They don't believe I'm doing anything about this problem."

"I need you in office. I can't work with anyone else."

"Thanks for your vote of confidence, Freddy."

"Let's fix things."

"Launching the *Protectress* will help." Then, seeming to think aloud, she said, "It could let them know that you're not just sitting around, thinking things up. It could eliminate some of the fear of a little boy having all this power if they knew you trusted me and the teams, that you're following our advice, and that you look up to us as role models. We need to get the media up on the *Protectress* too. If we stop at the first part and can't complete the second, then we're all in trouble."

"I won't let anything stop me from bringing out the big guns. Don't worry."

"I won't."

"Then this is what we can do." Our discussion lasted until the food was ready, and then we signed off, and I ate my dinner. Then it was off to bed for some much-needed rest. We were tired.

✦

Little Yellows said to me, "Gray seems to be upset about your people grabbing our information."

I answered, *"Remind him that he is doing the same thing by probing me. What's a 'hordslowat'?"*

Little Yellows laughed, "A hordslowat is a small creature that steals food if you're not watching close enough. It became famous when an entire division went hungry due to lack of food and had to subsist on only rations for over a year. And the rations kept coming up missing, so the fleet had to make a trip over six million light–years home, just to get food."

I smiled. *"We have the same thing on our planet. We call them chipmunks."*

Meanwhile, Green said to Gray, "You are upset that all our information is compromised. Did you not think that maybe they got the idea from us?"

Gray stopped his pacing, his mouth dropped open, and his face elongated into what had to be an expression of complete shock. "Are you going insane?"

Green answered thoughtfully, "I don't think so. I will have myself checked, as it does run in my litter. However, do you not think that the creatures would see our stealing their people and taking information from their minds against their will as nearly the same thing?"

Gray was about to blast Green but stopped long enough to think. "I suppose they would. I know I would. They adapt quickly, don't they?"

Little Yellows said, "Too quickly. Please continue."

CHAPTER 32

✦ ✦ ✦

TO THE WORLD

The day of the press conference came quickly. Colleen woke me with, "Freddy, time to get up."

"Okay. In a few hours."

"No. Right now, young man. After breakfast it will be time to go to the press conference."

"Okay," I said grudgingly. I took a shower and washed really good. I even washed my hair and used my powers to dry it, and then Colleen braided it nicely. We went down to breakfast, and I had oatmeal with cinnamon, sugar, and milk—good stuff. Then it was back up to my bedroom to get dressed. Colleen helped me, and I put on my fancy suit with the vest the townspeople gave me. It's very nice and feels great, almost relaxing. It's made of a soft, smooth wool, dark blue with darker blue trim, and a black belt. It has a dark red vest with gold trim and a dark red-and-gold tie. I even have black leather shoes.

I took out a matching set of earrings, necklace, and bracelet. Colleen nearly fainted when she saw it. She helped me put the earrings on with trembling hands.

"Where did you get these?" she asked.

"One of my first inventions allowed me to find minerals

and precious stones. During summer vacation, Dad and I found a hidden treasure in a cavern in Tibet. I brought it out and took only this set as a finder's fee. The country allowed me to have them. Nice, aren't they?"

"Are they real rubies?"

"No. They're perfect red diamonds. There are twenty-seven stones in each earring, including the thumb-sized one in the center. The bracelet has the same number only larger, as you can see, and the same with the necklace, except the center stone in the necklace is fist-sized. I was going to give the set to Mother, but she died before I could. I won't wear a necklace, as it could easily get caught in some of the moving parts of my work, so I only wear the earrings. I like the teardrop shape, but the set gets heavy after a while. I think that's mostly because of the twenty-four-carat gold filigree surrounding everything. I fell in love with them the first time I saw them. Does the red go well with the suit?"

"You look like an angel. Yes, the red looks great with the suit. Go downstairs now, and see the captain. I need to get ready."

I headed downstairs and received compliments from everyone about my hair and earrings. When Maggie saw my earrings, she immediately started working on the computer. While I was talking to Captain James, Maggie came in with a printout on the earrings I was wearing.

"Interesting," the captain said, She turned to me and asked, "Do you happen to have the rest of that set?"

"Yes, I do."

"Did you know your set has a name and history?"

"Really?"

She handed me the printout Maggie had showed her and said, "Those earrings are priceless. Please take them off, and put them away."

"But—"

"No 'buts,' young man. They do go well with the suit, but they would bring unwanted attention to you and your home. That set belongs in a museum."

"Oh man," I whined, but I traipsed upstairs and put them away. I put in my favorite pair of earrings, the ones with the bells that Becky gave me.

"That's much better," Susan said when I came back downstairs. "Is everyone ready?" She received affirmatives around the room. "Then let's go." We headed outside where we climbed into one of the shuttles and took off, followed by six Stingers.

"Where's the other shuttle?" I asked.

"Picking up the president. She should already be there."

"Nice. Why the escorts?"

"For show."

It took only two minutes to get to Crescent City, which is south of my home. We landed in the parking lot of the Del Norte County fairgrounds. Time to put on my sad face. Everyone else put on their "if looks could kill" faces, and out we went. When the crowd saw us getting out, they started pushing in, and then they saw our faces and backed up quickly.

I slowly walked into the main building and up to the makeshift stage. I sat down, still looking sad and hurt. I was, so it wasn't hard to look that way. The president came over to me and tried to wipe tears from my eyes, but I pulled my face away. She looked scared.

The president approached the podium and said, "Ladies and gentlemen, Freddy has something to say." She stepped down, looking worried, and I stepped up.

I looked out at the audience and at the cameras and said, "Why do you persecute me? What have I done to deserve all the hate mail you send me? My hair is long for two reasons: One, I can heal with my mind, and the energy in my hair allows me to heal more people. If I cut it short, I would possibly take away some of my ability to help others in an emergency. Believe me, if I could cut it short, I would. It's a mess to take care of. Two, my mother and father, God rest their souls, had long hair, and both wore earrings. I just like to be the way I want. The way my mother and father were. And again I say, so what? I don't see the problem. Why do you hate me?" Tears were streaming down my cheeks.

I turned to the captain and, in such a way that the microphones could pick it up, I said very sadly, "I want to go home now." I stepped off the podium and started to walk away. The president took hold of me and pulled me to her. She talked to me for a few seconds, saying things like, "Sweetheart, they don't all hate you. It's only a few people. Everyone knows people who are like that. It can't be helped." The microphones were picking up her comments really well.

I kept playing along. "I know, but it hurts so much. I don't hate people just because they don't do what I would do. That's so silly and sad."

The entire crowd of thousands was silent as they listened.

"Look, sweetheart," the president went on. "I love you, and these girls love you."

I threw my arms around her and hugged her, saying, "I love you too. I'm so glad you're the president."

She said, "We all love you, dear. Now let's dry those tears. I'll bet the crowd here loves you too." A cheer of thousands of voices of praise and love came up in an instant. I turned slightly toward the crowd, and the president said, "Freddy, they need your help. They're all going to die if you don't help."

I think it was the first time that had been said publicly. The entire crowd—and as I was told later, nearly the entire world—was quiet for that minute between what she said and my next words.

"I don't want anyone to be hurt. I'll help. I have just the thing to do that," I said with a solemn, slow nodding of my head.

"I know, dear, but they need to know so they can sleep at night."

"I hate it when I can't sleep. I get up and work instead. Don't they?"

"Some do, dear, but not like you." She took my hand, and we went back to the podium. "I want everyone to know what this child has been doing. He goes to work for three and four days straight—no sleep, no food. When he comes out of his workshop, he gets a quick meal and then goes to bed. After catching a little sleep, he starts all over. He's been on this schedule for years. He found out about the 'rock,' as he calls it, and decided to dedicate his life to catching and destroying it, and now he's just about ready. I've promised him a trip to Disney World after that rock is destroyed."

I looked at her and asked, "Can I see the Smithsonian too, please?"

"I think that can be arranged, sweetheart," she said with a smile.

The lieutenant stepped in and added, "He has something he wants to donate to a good museum."

The president turned back to the audience and said, "He's tired, worn out, his nerves are on edge, he's had no playtime or childhood to speak of, and thinks only of protecting you so that no one gets hurt. He gets no pay for this but does it out of the kindness of his heart. I am totally disgusted with anyone who would dare send hate mail to a child, especially a child who is trying to save the world from total destruction. With the help of this child, the United States will save the world, and we will do so while protecting our own natural resources. Freddy is one of our most precious resources, as are all of our children." She said this with so much emotion I was astonished to feel that she truly believed everything she said.

The crowd nearly went wild with cheers. It took a lot of time to calm them down. Finally, they did quiet down so that questions could be asked. The first question came from a pretty girl who was a reporter.

"We have been told that all the nuclear missiles in the entire world cannot stop this 'rock,' so how can you?"

"Oh, it was very hard. I wanted to invent ships to take me to the moon and Mars to set up stop-off places to new planets. I made them military-style ships so that they could help me bust up the rock and send it away."

The same reporter continued. "They say that what we've seen so far of your ships, even though they are wonderful and beyond anything we could have dreamed possible, do not have the power at this time to destroy the rock. Is this right?"

"Oh, those are only toys. I've just finished the real ship. Want to see it? As soon as I get back home, we're taking it out on a trial run." That caused a lot of murmurs, and the crowd had to be quieted down again.

"Yes. We'd love to see it. Are you inviting us to come to your home?"

"After the captain has screened you. Sure. My friends have told me that you've been very helpful and that I should be nice in return. Want to come over for lunch? My cook is really great. We could have a party." I looked at the captain, and she nodded her head before walking up to the podium.

"We'll take Freddy back home and then return in the shuttle with the equipment to scan the minds of anyone who wants to come home with us. Be ready to answer some very personal questions, and be very truthful, as we will evict anyone who even slightly shows up as hiding something. Your equipment will be scanned, and any weapons will be destroyed—along with anyone trying to bring them in. Make sure you know your camera crew very well. Your life depends on it."

"That sounds a little severe, Captain," said someone from the crowd.

"It is. If you had to protect the only chance for the survival of the human race, I think you'd be doing the same or more."

"Just to let you know," said the president, "every time I visit Freddy's home, I get the same treatment, as do all of my people. I almost lost two generals because I did not tell the captain's team that they were coming along. Freddy's guards do not like surprises. Every one of us had guns pointed at our heads, with fingers on the triggers. The security is tight, and it stays that way. The orders are simple: anyone trying to do anything even the least bit suspicious will die. In this situation, we have no choice. I fall under those orders, and so will any reporters."

"Are you taking any other countries' personnel up with you on this flight?" a reporter asked.

"There will be plenty of time for politics and letting the world in on the fun of going to other worlds, but in this case, no one not already cleared by NASA and the NSA will come close to this ship. No special rides, no free rides, no politics. The success of this mission is too important."

I leaned in as if I wanted to speak, and the president let me. "I do think we need a couple of good, honest reporting firms to go along. Someone needs to document what is done and that the rock is definitely destroyed. The captain will look into that. Right, Captain?"

"Yes, I will."

Another reporter asked, "Then there's room for reporting teams?"

"Wait 'til you see her," I said. "She can hold a crew of five hundred or so."

Another murmur went through the crowd.

The captain said, "Last question."

The lady reporter asked, "What is the name of the ship?"

The president answered. "They named her Earth ship *Protectress*."

We left after a lengthy standing ovation.

✦

Gray said, "Did we not destroy a ship called *Protectress*?"

I said through little Yellows, "Yes, you did, you murderer!"

Everyone was shocked, even little Yellows. They said, "We told you to hurry up. He is very strong."

Blue started to say something, but Green cut in. "I know. Continue."

CHAPTER 33

✦ ✦ ✦

PLAYING BALL

We quickly came back to the base with the president. She received a call saying her polls had gone through the roof. The election was next month, and all of a sudden she was very popular, even more so now that the world knew that she and I got along really well.

At home, everyone was waiting. I changed into something a bit more proper for the mission and a television appearance. It took an hour for the two press crews to arrive. While I waited, I went inside my workshop and fetched my new ball. Then I came out and familiarized myself with the people who were going to pilot the *Protectress*. They were a good lot. Almost all of them had come off an aircraft carrier called the *America*. The captain and the crew had received training from our girls. A few were from NASA, including the navigator and the science officer. The admiral was coming with us as Admiral of the Fleet. It was all exciting and fun. I took them into the workshop and down into the construction area. They were astounded but did everything I asked of them and went right to work in the *Protectress*. They were nice enough to leave everything else alone.

I mentioned to the admiral and the president, "It sure will be nice when I can get some help with my building-mover."

The admiral said, "Freddy, all the help you could ever want is waiting for you to just say the word."

The camera crew arrived. It was a completely mixed group from the "Big Five." Some reporters did not make the cut, and some camera people didn't either, so they combined those who did into one group. Helping each other was new to them, but they were enjoying it. I tossed the ball back and forth with a couple of the reporters. The one who had the ball was allowed to ask a question. They enjoyed that too.

We had a good lunch, and there were hundreds more questions. Enough equipment was brought in to make it a live broadcast, and I added some abilities to help them stay live, even in space. The first question was, "Why did you change your clothes?"

I answered, "Lack of gravity can make clothes ride way up, and I didn't want to have my tie in my face if the antigravity units faulted."

Two of the ladies on the media crews, including one butter-fingered reporter who'd dropped the ball, asked the captain if there were any extra coveralls they could use. Susan sent them into one of the small homes and let them change.

When it was time to depart, I went back into the workshop with the admiral, the president, Susan, two guards who flanked me (of course), and the media. They were allowed to take pictures and did so quietly. When they were aboard and in their seats on the bridge, I checked a few things and then took the security clamps off the computer.

✦

Blue said, "Nice of him to help the president that way."
Little Yellows said, "He is a nice creature."
I said, "Thank you."
Green panicked and said, "Everyone, shut up, please!"

CHAPTER 34

✦ ✦ ✦

MAIDEN FLIGHT OF THE PROTECTRESS

I said, "The *Protectress's* computer is named Gal."

In a nice second soprano voice, Gal said, "*Good afternoon, Freddy.*"

"Good afternoon, Gal. How are you doing?"

"*I have run a class-one diagnostics, and I am working at 100 percent across the board.*"

"Good, Gal. Please inform me if there is any change that will require my attention. As you can see, you now have a crew."

"*Yes. Good afternoon, President Kabe. It's nice to have you aboard. I will take good care of you.*"

"Thank you, Gal."

"*Good afternoon, Fleet Admiral Pinn. Welcome aboard.*"

"Hello, Gal. It's nice to be here."

"*Hi, Captain Rex. Nice to see you again.*"

"Nice to be on board at last."

"Gal, as set up before, I am turning over control to Captain Rex. Please give him all the information and control he needs to run the *Protectress*."

"Control exchange completed. Orders, Captain?"

"Gal, I know you can probably do this better than we can, and please keep training the crew, but I want the crew to have hands-on practice running your systems, so please give over control to the people on this list as stated." He held up a crystal and put it in the slot in his chair-side console.

"Information downloaded, and personnel recognized and confirmed in position."

"Gal, warn us if we're making any mistakes in navigation or protocol."

"Confirmed."

"Good. Engineering?"

Over the speakers, we heard, "On line, Captain."

"Power her up."

"Coming up to full power in five, four, three, two … at full power, Captain. Everything's green."

"Navigator, take us out into the open."

"Aye-aye, Captain. Shop, please open the bay doors."

"Bay doors opened."

"Science confirms the bay doors are open, Captain."

"Navigation, shields up."

"Shields up and working."

"Captain, scans show eight ships waiting to accompany us."

"Understood."

I placed my ball next to me at just above head level. It floated there on its own power. I drifted off for a while, thinking of several improvements I could make.

"Take us out, Navigator."

"Antigravity on. Bringing her up two feet and leveling off. Gal, report please."

"All systems normal. No abnormal structural stresses."

I broke in. "Gal, please send all reports to my console. I would like to analyze them."

"Compliance, Freddy."

I studied the readouts while the rest of the crew flew the ship. Science was watching the reports too, but they had other jobs to do, and I wanted the reports closely watched. I hoped that there would be no major mistakes.

"Bring her up to forty feet and turn her over."

We could watch what was happening on the screen, and we raised up and did a 360. The camera crew was astonished, saying things like, "I felt nothing, not even in my stomach," and "The gravity stayed the same. This is amazing." Susan told them to hold it down.

"Maneuver completed."

"Forward antigravity engaged at twenty feet per minute."

We were moving forward slowly but still forward. One of the reporters asked the president, "Why are we moving so slowly?"

She whispered to him, "They're testing out the controls and getting a feel for her. In addition, since she's never been flown, they're checking her out. Everything must work and work correctly before she can be used for FTL flight. Testing a new ship is probably more dangerous than anything you could ever imagine."

I interjected, "Wanna bet?"

She frowned at me and continued. "Any one thing goes wrong, and this whole ship could smash us all to pulp."

The reporter nervously asked, "Has Freddy been putting his life on the line like this a lot?"

"Every hour of every day. Gal, please contact Shop."

"Completed."

"Shop?"

"Yes, Madam President."

"How many times has Freddy come close to death while working on this project?"

"Eighteen thousand four hundred five times, not counting what he's doing now."

"Shop!" I said as a warning.

"My goodness!" exclaimed the reporter.

The president said, "You don't think this kind of technology comes without risks, do you? Freddy loves people, and he hates to think of people being harmed. He wants to go to the moon and then Mars and build a home in outer space. He figures that he could safely have the first ship built in about five years, but the rock and our peril has been his first priority. He has spent the last few years building this ship, and it came with costs. For instance, no childhood, loss of his first love, continuous heartbreaking work, and nearly killing himself to complete every part of the project."

"He's a remarkable boy."

I broke in and said, "Hey. You're embarrassing me. Please stop. Besides, God helped."

They stared at me for a minute, and then one reporter asked, "You talk to God?"

"No, I pray to God for guidance, and I get some remarkable ideas. I'm content with getting inspiration."

They both relaxed a little.

"He has strong faith, as you can see," said the president. She turned to the screen and said, "Time to watch." We were just leaving the home base and going up through the shields.

"Home base cleared. We have confirmation and clearance to proceed, Captain."

"How are you feeling, Gal?"

"Fine, Captain. No issues except a crack in a weld in section 3.1.2.5."

I said, "That would be forward section, level one, at point two, and five feet in from starboard. Captain, please hold while I check that out."

"Holding, Freddy."

Patricia and I left the quarterdeck and headed forward and down to level one. On the way, she asked, "What's the deal with the ball?"

"Tell no one, but it's the answer." She didn't ask any more, but I could tell she now was really curious.

When we reached the forward deck, Gal led us to the issue. Sure enough, one of the welds on the forward laser cannon was weak and cracked. "Okay, Patricia. You know the drill. This is only the first." She smiled, and we worked together using a tractor beam to pull the cannon back into place and then using a die-breaker to remove and remake the seam completely. When we were finished, we scanned it to ensure its completeness. Everything was good to go, and Gal reported that to the bridge. When we returned, they were already at twenty-five miles straight up and getting ready to test the impulse engines. We took our seats. I checked the ship's systems, and I checked the ball. Everything was green.

"Gal," said Captain Rex, "status, please."

"All is working at optimum, Captain."

"Navigator, plot a course that will take us out of this solar system with no obstacles."

"Scanning. Plotting. Laid in, Captain."

"Start at one hundred miles per hour. Engage."

The screen showed forward, aft, and eight other positions. We could clearly see Earth, and at this range, we could hardly tell we were moving.

"Scan reports one hundred miles per hour, Captain."

Captain Rex said, "Didn't feel a thing. Navigator, go to five hundred miles per hour. Engage."

"Scan reports five hundred miles per hour, Captain."

"Navigator, one-quarter impulse. Engage."

"Structural shift in sections 2.2.6 through 2.2.9."

"Captain," I said, "please hold at one-quarter impulse while I check this out."

"Will do, Freddy."

"Gal, show reports of structures surrounding sections 2.2.5 through 2.2.10." The reports came up on the screen. There was no damage. "Good. Now give me a report on the balance of the dampeners and gravity-field calibrations, both before and after the last change in speed."

Two lists came up on the board. A lot of adjustments were out of place on the first section labeled "before" but only two in red on the one labeled "after." I smiled. My automatic adjustments were working. The ship had corrected over eight hundred minor adjustments. Two were out of adjustment too far to be automatically corrected.

I left the quarterdeck with Patricia, saying, "This will only take a minute ..." By the time I made it to Engineering, though, Ensign Jason Tam had already completed the adjustments. Patricia was ecstatic that her friend, a brilliant engineer from MIT, had been remotely watching my console and saw the problems I saw and adjusted them out. As we headed back to the bridge. I gave her a pat on the back for her good choice of personnel.

"Captain, please cut speed to five hundred miles per hour or less, and then increase to one-quarter impulse again."

"Navigator, engage."

"Scan shows five hundred miles per hour. Scan now shows one-quarter impulse at twenty-five million miles per hour."

The captain said, "I didn't feel a thing, Freddy. Good job!"

"Not me, Captain. Ensign Tam had it adjusted before

we got there. He's a good man. Patricia and I may steal him from you if you're not careful."

He smiled and mumbled, "Over my dead body. Navigator, one-half impulse. Engage."

One of the reporters asked, "Freddy, what would have happened if we had tried to go faster before realizing that things were out of adjustment?"

I answered with a smile and said as politely as I could, "The *things*, ma'am, were gravity-field balancing units. If we had tried warp speed with them out of balance, then you would be asking this question of God. Going from any speed into warp speed is about the most dangerous thing you will ever experience. Any one of a million little things can go wrong and leave you like mush on the wall. I really should show everyone my experiments with fruit. It's a good way to make applesauce."

The president said, "Freddy, don't be morbid." She took over the conversation, saying, "Actually, he's telling the truth. It is extremely dangerous, but then, so was sailing to the New World. Let's look at facts. If you count all the small ships, this is the fortieth ship Freddy has put up so far, and not one has been less than perfect."

"Navigator," said the captain, "full impulse. Engage."

"Scan shows full impulse at 382.5 million miles per hour, Captain."

"Captain," said Communications. "*America's Pride* confirms 382.5."

"Very well. Log it in." He turned to me and said, "Slightly bigger, Freddy. That's a good hundred million faster than any other ship in the fleet."

I blushed and shrugged. "There's a lot more room on this ship, Captain. Therefore, I gave you some slightly oversized engines."

"Okay, Freddy. Any surprises with the FTL drive?"

"Oh yes. Just wait and see. You're going to like this."

He turned back around. "Here we go, folks. Navigator, give me warp one. Engage."

My stomach felt like it was going to turn inside out, and then everything settled. Ball looked upset too, so I picked it out of the air and whispered to it that everything was okay. It calmed down. The president saw me talking to the ball, so I asked her to hold it for me. "It gets nervous," I explained.

She smiled and said, "Gladly." She took the ball and started tossing it up about a foot and catching it.

I immediately turned to my console and started working on the problem. Nothing was wrong. There was no problem with the ship. "Gal, play back a scan of the navigational controls during that last move, include heading, expected position, and actual position." It came up on my screen. I studied it for a good minute before I saw the problem. "Captain, all stop, please."

"Navigator, engage." We came to a dead stop.

"Captain Rex, this is *America's Dream.*"

The captain said, "Put them on screen, Lieutenant Williams."

I waved hello to Lieutenant Morgan, as she was commanding *America's Dream.*

"Hi, Freddy. Captain Rex, that was a unique maneuver. Spinning faster than the speed of light. Add a little soap and water, and you'd be squeaky clean."

I went to the navigation station with Patricia and started pulling off a panel. Patricia asked, "What did you find, Freddy?"

"The navigational controls are off by nearly one-half of a percent on the Z-axis and over two percent on the Y-axis."

She said, "I'll get the Y-axis, then." She started taking off another panel. We were both deep inside the navigation station and passing tools back and forth as the captains talked. When we finished, we put everything back together and cleaned up. We inventoried the tools and sat down. It's not good to have loose tools around. I found that out the hard way.

"Captain," I said, "if you would please."

"Navigator, five hundred miles per hour."

"Captain," I interrupted, "please go to warp one right off."

"From a dead stop, Freddy? I thought you said that we should not do that."

"Surprise! With this new engine it's no longer an issue outside of atmosphere."

"Very well. Navigator, warp one. Engage." We hit warp one as smooth as could be.

"Scan reports warp one, Captain."

"Good job, Patricia and Freddy. You're a good team."

"Thanks," we said in unison.

"Navigator, let's have warp two. Engage."

Scan said, "Captain, at warp two on this new course, we will hit several objects in twenty seconds."

"Scan reports at warp two, Captain."

"Navigator, set in a course around those objects. Engage."

"New course laid in and engaged, sir."

"Scan shows a clear path again, sir."

"Bring the objects up on the screen." The screen showed several parts of an alien ship. There were burn spots, indicating signs of a conflict.

The admiral said, "Captain, order two ships to stay back and scan that wreck. I want to know what did this and how, who that ship belonged to, and why it was left out here. Freddy, do you need the parts off that thing?"

"No, sir. My scanners show it's all common stuff. All well below our technology."

"Then after making a complete report, get rid of it. I don't want debris cluttering up our space. Make it so, Comms."

The captain shifted in his seat. "Okay. Now let's see what this baby can do. Navigator, warp eight. Engage."

"Coming to warp eight now, sir."

We were flying now.

The captain asked, "Freddy, the controls at Navigation are only halfway. Why?"

I turned around and faced him. "Surprise again, Captain! Try warp ten."

He looked at me skeptically. "Navigator, warp ten. Engage."

"Coming to warp ten in three, two, one. Warp ten, Captain."

"You may be able to squeeze warp 10.5 out of them," I said, "but be careful, and don't stay at it for very long."

"Freddy, you're amazing."

I smiled. "Thanks."

He turned around and said, "Navigator, warp five, please. Let's give the others a chance to catch up."

"Where are we, Freddy?" asked a reporter.

"Well past Pluto and close to Alpha Centauri."

The crew played "chase" and "tag" for three hours with the rest of the fleet before starting for home.

✦

Gray said in amazement, "His first big ship could do warp ten!"

I giggled, as little Yellows was tickling me to keep me quiet.

Green said, "Apparently they started out faster than we did."

Yellows asked, "What is the ball for?"

Green smiled behind a tentacle. "It's the answer, Yellows."

"Funny, Green. Continue."

CHAPTER 35

SAVING THE WORLD
IN TWO WAYS

The captain turned his chair around. "Dr. Anderson?"
"Whoops, using my title. Something important, Captain?"

"Yes, Freddy. When can we destroy that rock?"

"Actually, I'm glad you asked. I'm ready now, if you are."

"How long will it take to load your equipment, sir?" the captain asked.

"On this console, two minutes at the most," I said.

"Don't we have to go back to the base and get your missiles?"

"I need only one."

Everyone straightened in his or her seat, and the tension escalated.

"Only one, Freddy?"

"The improvements made to this ship, Captain, and the fact that we have a fleet of forty ships assisting makes it necessary to only break it into smaller pieces. After that, it will be target practice for the fleet. Captain, nothing must escape. If some pieces are allowed to hit our asteroid belt, then you guys could be kept busy for a very long time. For that reason, I made one missile that pretty much removes most of it, all at once."

"Understood. Navigator, lay in a course for that rock at warp five. Engage. Communications, have the fleet join us there. Freddy, just for my understanding, how far back would you suggest we be when your missile goes off?"

I turned to my console and did some figuring. "About half a light-year, and be prepared to start shooting the pieces that break off. Please have the shields up to full, Captain. The shock wave could be bad."

"Where are all the rest of the missiles?"

"All of the information and all of the other missiles have been dismantled, and the component parts were used to build this ship." I shrugged and said, "I was running out of available materials, Captain. I spent a few minutes thinking of where I could get some. They were the best choice; therefore, I changed the design and made one simple missile capable of doing all the work by itself, and I used the leftover materials to help build the last parts for the engines on this ship." I smiled.

"Good thinking, Freddy. But what happens if that missile misses?"

"It won't miss, Captain."

"Humor me, Freddy. What happens?"

"This missile is for that rock, and if it misses, the most likely thing will be that it will be pulled into the sun or the gravitational pull of another planet."

"And …?"

"No more sun or planet."

A cameraman exclaimed. "That's not possible. You can't destroy the sun with one simple missile. It's pure nuclear power."

"My bomb does not work on normal thinking, sir. I

assure you that if it aimed its sights at the sun, then the sun would be gone from existence."

The president asked nervously, "And a thing like that is on this ship?"

"You're holding it."

"Quit kidding with me, Freddy."

"Bomb, come here, please."

The ball drifted up from her lap and came over to me. "It's totally harmless until I arm it. See, Madam President?" I tossed it up. The captain grabbed it and, very slowly and gently, set it down on his chair.

"Freddy, when we get back, I am going to give you a spanking myself," said the president, shaking.

One of the reporters fainted. I said, "Whoops. I think she just remembered that she dropped the ball." As they were taking care of her, I said, "Look, Madam President—I couldn't just leave it alone. I had to bring it with us, as it gets upset when it's left alone for very long. Its computer is very touchy." I turned toward the ball and said, "Bomb, come here, please." It drifted up and over to me. "It's all right. They don't hate you. Calm down, please."

"Captain, we're at station. Twenty-one of the smaller ships are with us. The rest that we can man are on the way."

"Good," I said. "Everyone ready?"

The captain gave orders to the fleet to spread out and surround the rock at one-half light-year. "Nothing gets through," he ordered. When all forty ships were ready, he turned to me. "Please, Freddy, get rid of that thing."

I think he was talking about the ball, but I purposefully took it to mean the asteroid. The rock was already on screen. I said, "Team, please pay no attention to what I'm about to say to Bomb." They nodded.

"Bomb?" I said. It blinked a little green. "See that rock on the screen?" It blinked green again. "Scan for it outside at about half a light-year away." It blinked blue and then green. "See it?" It blinked green. "That rock is going to harm me." It blinked red and disappeared—and so did the rock.

"Captain, scans show an energy wave heading out in all directions from where that rock was. It's traveling at warp 3.23. It's destroying everything in its path. It's diminishing, half strength, quarter strength, nearly gone. It's gone, sir."

"Scan the area for debris."

"Yes, Captain, scanning. No debris at all, Captain. Not even the normal space dust. Nothing." Admiral Pinn turned toward me, staring.

Everyone was looking at me. Communications ended the silence. She said, "Captain, all ships are reporting the same thing. Look at the scans. They're doing loops—and listen to this, sir." She put the ship's intercom on the speaker. There was yelling and cheering and general "We did it!" throughout the ship. The captain gave the sign to have the speaker cut out, and all went silent. Susan pulled me to her, as she could see I was frightened by the attention I was getting. They were not cheering on the bridge.

I read their thoughts—just the surface ones—and so did Melanie, the president's aide. She turned to me and said, "Freddy, you know why they're so worried, don't you?"

"I know."

"You know what you must do. I can read you very clearly, and it's the right thing."

"I know, but I'm scared."

"We'll protect you, but you must do it."

I looked at her, and before Susan could ask what I was going to do, I put my hand to my head. I screamed and screamed and finally passed out. The bridge was now in turmoil. The captain got things under control quickly and said, "Please tell me our hero is still alive."

I was bleeding from my mouth, eyes, nose, and ears. Susan said, "He has a pulse, but it's faint. Melanie, what did he do?"

"He's all right, Captain James. It just hurts." She had tears in her eyes. "It hurts more than anything you can possibly imagine. Luckily, he passed out quickly. If he had not, he could have died from the pain. He'll be okay in a few days. Very tired and weak but okay."

"What did he do?"

Melanie looked up with tears pouring from her eyes. "He did something harder to do than anything he has ever done. He gathered all knowledge on how to build that bomb and literally burned it out of his mind. His last thoughts before passing out were of the president, Becky, Susan, and his girls."

A reporter solemnly asked, "What were his thoughts?"

"'Because I love you all.'"

I woke up in my own bed back at home. Becky was there by my bedside, and so were Susan and Katie. Becky and Susan each had one of my hands. As my eyes opened and focused, Susan said, "Welcome back, sweetheart."

I tried to talk, but Becky placed a finger on my lips and said, "Not yet, dear. In a few days." I tried to sit up, but my head hurt so much I couldn't move.

Susan said, "You're not getting up or doing anything for a while, so get used to it."

I was so tired I wasn't about to complain. There was a intravenous feed going into my arm, and a person I hadn't seen before was watching us. She pathed to me, *"Hi, Freddy. I'm your nurse. My name is Sally. Don't try pathing back. You can receive easy enough, but sending will be hard for a while. Let your brain rest, and let me heal you."* I nodded my head a little and winced.

Sally said, "You've all seen him awake. Now, out. He needs rest. Out!" She saw how my hand clamped a little on Becky's hand, and she smiled. "Not you, Becky. You can stay." They left, and Sally came over to me and said, "Sleep, little one. And thank you for getting the president to find me." I received an impression of a young lady in an asylum, afraid that she could hear voices and being kept drugged.

I looked at Becky and smiled, and then I turned to Sally. I tried to say, "How many like you?" But she put her hand on my head. Just before I fell asleep, she whispered, "Hundreds, Freddy. Hundreds."

✦

Yellows asked, "Wasn't our mother ship cloaked as an asteroid?"

Green sadly said, "Yes."

Yellows continued. "Did not Gray tell us that their scanners could not see through the cloaking device?"

Green, almost in shock, said, "Yes, he did."

Blue asked, "Is this not about the time transmissions stopped from our mother ship?"

Green choked out, "It is the exact time."

Little Yellows said to me, *"It is not your fault. You could not know, little one."*

Green pulled out of the link. "I cannot continue until he stops crying. This realization is literally killing him."

Blue said, "Yellows, please have your pen mate work with him. This was not his fault. This was bad planning on our part. I need to report. We will continue tomorrow."

Little Yellows answered, "We will do our best, but we do not think it will help."

Over the intercom, an alarm sounded, and a voice said,

"Attention, all ships. The Earth fleet has stopped and is turning around. We have one hour before they reach us. Prepare for battle."

To be continued ...

Printed in the United States
By Bookmasters